PICTURE PERFECT COWBOY

TIFFANY REISZ

8TH CIRCLE PRESS

AUTHOR'S NOTE

A heavily abridged version of PICTURE PERFECT COWBOY was previously published in the limited-edition EXPOSED anthology as the novella "The Watermark" (now out of print).

1

The list of things Jason would rather be doing that day was as long as his arm. In no particular order he'd rather be:

Mucking out the stalls.

Mowing the lawn.

Re-shingling the roof.

Repainting the barn.

Cleaning the gutters.

Having his head examined.

Any of those would be a lot easier than what he was doing now.

How in the hell had he let Luke talk him into this? Stripping down bare-ass naked for a calendar shoot? And for a literary charity? Did that make any damn sense? What books and naked men had to do with each other he didn't know and probably never would. But he'd told Luke he'd do it so here he was, doing it.

"Luke, if this goes viral," Jason muttered to himself, "you're a dead man."

Jason could only hope and pray his mother didn't find out about this. He was number one on her shit list already for moving halfway across the country. If she found out her baby boy was baring all for the whole world to see, she'd fly all the way from Montana to Kentucky just to tell him he'd broken her heart and shamed the family name. And his father would drive there for the pleasure of dragging him behind the nearest woodshed. Didn't matter he was twenty-nine years old. Dad would tan his hide worse than the time he put a garter snake in his sister's underwear drawer when he was seven.

And he'd probably deserve it.

The drive to the Bourbon County Public Library only took about half an hour but Jason managed to stretch it out to thirty-five by laying off the gas. He didn't want to get there early. He didn't want to be late either. What he wanted was to get it over with as soon as possible, and then pretend this whole stupid thing had never happened.

Until the calendars came out, of course, and everyone and their grandmother knew what his ass looked like.

Jason tried not to think about that part as he pulled into the library parking lot. He parked, turned off his truck, grabbed his hat off the seat, and got out, trying hard not to slam the door behind him. He mostly succeeded. His truck, a red Ford older than he was, needed a little extra elbow grease to get the door to latch. Least that's what excuse he gave himself for hitting the door a little harder than necessary.

He was supposed to ask for a gal named Simone. Apparently, she was the photographer they'd hoodwinked into flying all the way down to Kentucky to take his picture. Luke also told him to "be nice," which Jason had taken as a personal slight. When had Luke ever known Jason Waters to be rude to a woman? Not her fault he didn't want to do this, he told Luke. Luke's fault, maybe.

Maybe definitely.

Jason took the library's front steps two at a time. With one hand he opened the glass door and with the other he removed his hat. The librarian at the front desk smiled at him in greeting. He gave her a smile back that he hoped didn't look as fake as it felt. If he'd been on his way to the firing squad, he might have smiled the same way.

He mentally added *standing in front of a firing squad* to his list of things he'd rather be doing that day.

Unfortunately, Luke hadn't told him where to go once he got to the library, which meant he had to ask. He walked up to the desk and started to make a fool of himself by asking where he was supposed to go to get naked pictures of himself taken when he heard a woman's soft voice behind him.

"Are you Jason Waters?"

He turned and came face to face with a woman who had to be this New York photographer Luke told him about.

For starters, the girl had pink hair. All pink. Cotton candy pink and curling around her smiling face. She also had tattoos on both arms and a ring in her nose. If she was a local, he was Garth Brooks.

"I am, ma'am. Are you Miss Levine?"

"Simone, please," she said. "And I think that's the first time I've ever been ma'amed in my life."

She grinned at him, and even with all the crazy colored hair and the ring in her nose, Jason had to admit to himself she was a pretty lady. Bright smiling eyes. Good full lips. And in her tight jeans and white t-shirt that rode high enough he could see three or four inches of soft pale belly, he could tell she had a really nice figure. Not that he wanted to notice any of that if he was taking his clothes off for her. There was a time and place for enjoying a woman's curves, and naked in front of a camera for a charity calendar was not the time or the place.

"Habit," he said. "If you don't like it, I'll try not to do it again. But if I slip, I apologize."

"It's all right," she said, smiling even wider. He must have amused her though he had no idea how or why. "I kind of like it. Are you ready? I have the room all set up."

Jason took a deep breath and gestured with his hat for her to lead the way.

"We really appreciate you agreeing to be in the calendar," she said as they walked past stacks of books and up the stairs to the second floor. "Can I call you Jason or do you prefer Mr. Waters?"

"Call me whatever you like," he said.

"Luke Bradley was supposed to be our Mister November," she said. "But he's having some kind of surgery, right?"

Jason nodded. Luke had gotten thrown from a bull last month and slipped a disc in his back that needed correcting. He was in a Montana hospital right now, flirting with the nurses. Ah, could have been worse. Jason and Luke had both been pallbearers for fellow cowboys.

"It's nice of you to step in for him," she said. "He said you're prettier than he is anyway."

Jason laughed softly. "That's not saying much."

"He did tell me he's got more scar tissue than regular tissue on his body these days," Simone said. "What's that called? An occupational hazard?"

"You don't ride bulls if you want to stay pretty," Jason said.

"That why you quit?" she asked as they reached a set of dark wood double doors.

Jason shrugged. "Quit for a lot of reasons. Wanting to meet my grandkids was only one of them."

"Well, I read online you were the world champion two years in a row. Nothing wrong with going out on top."

Jason didn't say anything to that. He just opened the door for her.

"Not much of a talker, I see," Simone said as she stepped inside the room and waved her hand at two leather chairs sitting by a window.

"Not much to say," Jason said.

"Well, I'll do most of the talking," she said. "You want to sit?"

"After you."

She eyed him with a twinkle in her eyes.

"You are the real deal, aren't you?" she asked as she sat down in the nearest chair. He sat in the one opposite her, his dark brown cowboy hat on his knee. "Ma'am? Opening the door for me? Waiting for me to sit before you'll sit?"

Jason only smiled. If his parents had taught him anything worthwhile it was humility. And to keep his damn mouth shut if he didn't have anything to say.

"I was hoping we could talk a few minutes before we started the shoot," she said. "I know it's not easy taking your clothes off in front of a stranger. Especially when that stranger's holding a camera. I thought maybe we ought to get comfortable with each other first."

"Whatever you like."

"First, let me ask...do you really want to do this?" she asked.

"I said I would."

"That's not what I asked."

She sat back in the big chair and pulled her legs in and crossed them.

"I said I'd do it," Jason said. "And I do want to keep my word."

"I hope Luke Bradley didn't force you into this," she said.

He shook his head. "Luke couldn't force me into a pie-eating contest when I'm dying for pie. We're old friends," Jason said. "That's why I'm hard on him. He's a good man. If he thinks this is a cause worth his time, then it's worth mine."

Simone was still staring at him like he was some kind of alien. Maybe he was to a gal from New York with pink hair and a nose ring.

"These calendars raise a ton of money and awareness for their causes," she said. "You can't find a much better cause than literacy. It's very nice of you to agree to this even if you aren't in love with the idea."

"What gave it away?" he asked.

"You're about to destroy the brim of your hat," she said. "I hope that's crushable velvet you've been crushing for the past five minutes."

Jason looked down at his hat brim. She was right. He'd twisted it so hard it would have torn had it been made of any material other than crushable velvet. He laughed at himself and groaned quietly.

"Never done this sort of thing before," he said. "That's all."

"Getting naked for a stranger and getting

photographed is a big deal," she said. "It's not for everyone. And I can already tell you're kind of uncomfortable with it, which makes me uncomfortable. I like willing partners. Not people gritting their teeth the whole time."

"I'm here to do the job," he said. "I don't have to love it."

"This isn't a job, Jason. You're not getting paid."

"Still, I said I'd do it. I'll do it."

She looked at him without saying anything. Then she smiled again. He'd never expected a New Yorker to smile so much. He'd always heard they were tough cookies up there. Simone didn't seem like a tough cookie, though. More like bubblegum.

"Let me show you some of the pictures I've taken for previous calendars so you know what you're getting into. They're not X-rated, I promise. Pretty tame."

She picked up a leather binder from a bag next to the chair and flipped through some pages.

"You, uh, take a lot of pictures of naked men?" he asked.

"I have," she said. "I've done a couple different naked charity calendar shoots. You kind of have to have very special people skills for that job. And I've done a few boudoir shoots with women. And I do some fetish photography myself. I know what I'm doing. Usually."

"Interesting line of work you're in," he said.

"That's pretty rich coming from a professional bull rider."

"*Retired* professional bull rider," he said.

"Still."

"Can't argue," he said.

"Have you ever done any modeling before?" she asked.

"Not modeling," he said. "I wouldn't call it that. But you have to get your picture taken a lot when you're on the rodeo circuit. Interviews and that sort of thing. And, you know, some other stuff."

"Other stuff? Like what?" she asked.

Jason didn't like to talk about these things, but he didn't like being rude to a woman, either. And maybe she needed to know this stuff for her job.

"I did a thing," he said.

"A thing? What kind of thing?"

"You know Levi's?" he asked.

"Levi's the jeans? Yeah, I've heard of them," she said. He could tell she was trying not to laugh.

"They had these new style jeans with extra rivets. You know, for rough wear? They thought a bull rider was the right guy to show them off."

She narrowed her eyes at him. "Jason, you were a Levi's jeans model?"

"I guess you could say that," he said. "The ads were in some magazines."

"In magazines? Which magazines?"

"Oh, I dunno. A few of them. *Time*, I think. *Maxim*.

Details. Um...*Men's Health*. *People*. Is that what you mean by modeling experience?"

"I would say having a Levi's ad in *Time*, *Maxim*, *People*, *Details* and *Men's Health* counts as modeling experience, yeah. Anything else? Cover of *Vogue*, maybe? Calvin Klein underwear model? Victoria's Secret Angel?"

"Ah...Ford commercial," he said. Simone was, for some reason, rubbing her forehead. "I really liked their new F-150s so I agreed to do a few TV spots for them. I doubt you got 'em in New York, though."

"Levi's and Ford trucks. Those are major ad campaigns, Jason," she said. "Like...the most major."

He only shrugged. "Paid the bills."

She took a long deep breath. "Well," she said, "guess you're old hat at this then. Makes my job easier."

"Nah. Levi's and Ford wanted me to keep my clothes on. This is brand new to me. Just talk to me like I'm dumb as a box of rocks."

"All right," she said. "I can do that. Well..." She flipped through her portfolio to a different section and showed him a picture. "I was thinking of posing you like this," she said. He liked how professional she sounded. This wasn't some kind of joke or come-on to her. Just a job. Just a job like the jeans thing and the Ford commercials. "This is my friend Griffin. He was in a calendar a couple years ago."

She showed him the photograph of a tall, muscular guy with a tan, black armband tattoos, and a big grin on his face holding up a book called *The Red*.

"He an athlete?" Jason asked. He wasn't sure what he was supposed to say. He didn't go around eyeballing naked men that often. Though Simone was right. You could see his side, hip, and thigh but that was about it. Pretty tame stuff.

"Trust fund baby," Simone said. "But he does a ton of charity work. And he coaches a well-known roller derby team in New York. The theme of the calendar that year was Notable New Yorkers, and they were raising money for a new library in Queens."

Jason narrowed his eyes at the photograph. "Am I supposed to smile like that?" Jason wasn't much of a smiler, not when he was naked with a camera pointed at him.

"Griffin wasn't supposed to smile like that. He was supposed to be reading and looking serious. But his boyfriend made a joke off-camera, and I caught him mid-laugh. It was the best shot in the set so we ran it."

"All right," Jason said. "That's not too bad. Mom might let me come home for Christmas after all."

"Conservative family?" Simone asked.

"You could say that."

"And you're doing it anyway?"

"I guess I am."

"You sure about it?"

Was he sure? He'd told himself the only reason he'd agreed to take Luke's place in the calendar was because Luke had asked him. But maybe there was a little part of him that wanted to take a risk, to put a little distance between the person everyone thought he was and the real Jason Waters, whoever the hell that was.

"Sure as I'll ever be," he said.

She gave him that searching look, but didn't question him anymore. She flipped through her album and showed him a few more photos going in the calendar. A basketball player with the ball in one hand blocking the view of his business while in his other hand he held a copy of *The Basketball Diaries*. A famous quarterback had his helmet across his lap while he read *Friday Night Lights*.

"Thoughts?" she asked. "Any pose look better to you than the others?"

"The first one's fine. Just get me from the left, not the right. I got some scars."

"Not a problem. I'll get your good side," she said. "You have any questions?"

He shook his head.

"Nothing?" she said.

"Can we get this over with?" he asked.

"We can."

She looked at him again, another long searching look.

"If you want to call the whole thing off, say the word," she said.

"What word?" he asked, a dumb joke to hide his nerves.

"Hmm..." she said and smiled. "You own a horse?"

"Of course," he said. "I retired from bulls, not from horses."

"What's your horse's name?"

"Ah, the one I usually ride around the farm, he's called Rusty."

"Great," she said. "Rusty can be your safe word. Anytime you want to call the whole thing off, say 'Rusty' and I'll turn my back and you'll get dressed and leave right away, no hard feelings. It's only April and we don't have to get the photos to the printer for months. We can find another guy to take your slot if you decide this won't work for you."

"It's real nice of you to say all that," he said. "And I appreciate it. But I'd like to just get on with it if you don't mind."

Simone raised her hands in surrender. "You're the boss."

She stood up first, and a second later he followed.

"Bathroom's down the hall if you need to go. Nobody wants to be naked and have to pee at the same time. I've got a changing screen right here," she said, pointing at a three-panel screen set up in the corner. "There's a towel back there you can wrap around your waist. I'll turn my back while you drop the towel and get into position. I'll photograph you at this angle," she said, demonstrating with her own body the position he'd need to stand in while she took pictures. "Side view with your thigh kind of forward. If we're careful, I might not see anything you don't want me to see. Although I hope you won't be upset if I do. It's just a human body. We all have them. Our bodies are nothing to be ashamed of."

He gave her a slight smile as he went behind the screen. He felt stupid hiding to change when she'd be seeing what the good Lord gave him in two minutes anyway. Still, nice of her to try to make him feel more comfortable.

As he unbuttoned his checkered red and black shirt, he heard her giggle. It was a nice laugh, pretty and girlish. He didn't expect women with nose rings to laugh so cute. Clearly he needed to adjust his prejudices.

"Something funny?" he asked.

"Oh, nothing," she said.

"You sure?"

"I thought it was funny that I said 'Rusty' could be your safe word," she said.

"And why's that funny?"

"Because," she said, "you didn't ask me what a safe word is. You already knew."

2

Simone knew immediately she'd made a mistake by saying that. Behind the screen, Jason was silent. She couldn't even hear him moving around anymore.

"I'm sorry," she said quickly. "I didn't mean to imply anything. I just thought it was funny that, thanks to certain books and movies that will remain nameless, even cowboys in Kentucky know what safe words are."

Simone held her breath and listened, hoping and praying Jason was still undressing back there.

"Takes a lot to offend me," he said at last. "You're gonna have to try harder than that if you want to."

Simone breathed a sigh of relief.

"Good. And really, I am sorry. I didn't want to make you uncomfortable. Just the opposite. I'm used to joking around with my models. I forgot there for a second you're not the typical model I work with."

"It's all right."

Simone shook her head. Nice. Very nice. She was trying so hard to make the man more comfortable and she'd accidentally insinuated he was a secret freak. As she was a not-so-secret freak she had a bad habit of doing that sort of thing. She tended to assume most people were kinky in one way or another until proven vanilla. But if there was any man on earth who was vanilla, it was Jason "Still" Waters. Hell, the man was probably a virgin. That might explain how intense and uptight he was. She couldn't quite believe he'd agreed to pose nude for the calendar. His friend Luke had probably twisted his arm, guilted him into it. Hard to say no when your best friend calls you from his hospital bed and asks you to take his spot in a charity calendar.

She busied herself adjusting the lights and the drapes and everything she'd already adjusted to perfection as she waited for Jason to emerge. And she swore to herself she would not make this any weirder for him than it already was.

"This is a really pretty library," Simone said to cover her nervousness. "Old Carnegie Library. One of the few left in the country still used as a library, I saw. It was nice of them to let us shoot here."

"Can't believe they said yes," Jason said from behind the screen.

"I didn't quite tell them the full nature of the calendar. What's that old saying? Better to ask forgiveness than permission?"

"Something like that," he said. "Is this your first time in Kentucky?" He had a nice voice, low and steady without much of an accent. And unlike a lot of the athletes she'd photographed for last year's calendar, he didn't seem to have any interest whatsoever in talking about himself. Or talking much at all.

"Yeah," she said. "It's nice here. So many horse farms. You're new here, right? Luke said you left Montana a year ago. What brought you to Kentucky?"

"Those horse farms," he said. "I'm a trainer now. Easier to do here than in Montana."

"More horses here?"

"Warmer winters," he said simply. "Longer training season."

He stepped out from behind the screen with the towel wrapped around his waist.

"Where do you want me?" he asked.

Simone caught herself staring at him.

"It's not as bad as it looks," he said. "Like I said, just get my good side."

Jason had a surgical scar on his torso about a foot long, a ragged V-shape that curved from underneath his left bottom rib down to his left hip.

"Wow," she said. "Bull riding is even more dangerous than I thought."

"It's my shark bite," he said and smiled. "Kind of looks like it, right?"

He traced the V with his fingertip.

"Kind of," she said. "I'm guessing it wasn't a shark."

"Just a mean old bull with a nasty sharp horn."

"You were gored?"

"A little. They sewed me up all right. Where do you want me?" he asked again. *Subject raised. Subject discussed. Subject dismissed.* She'd had longer conversations with baristas when ordering coffee than she did with this man about his life-threatening injuries.

"Um...here," she said and stood on a taped X on the floor, "if you want to stand. If you decide you'd rather sit, we can pull the chair over. And you'll need a book. I picked out a few from the shelves. I went for a Western theme. I've got *The Ox-Bow Incident*. I found a hardcover of *Lonesome Dove. All the Pretty Horses* by Cormac McCarthy. Any of those sound good?"

"I'm a Kentucky boy now. Let's see what they got here," he said and walked over to the bookcase. They were in the Kentucky Room of the library, a private study room that had to be reserved in advance. Nice room with a fireplace and glass-front barrister bookcases. But it wasn't the nice room Simone was staring at as Jason studied the bookshelves. Apart from the large scar, Jason had a gorgeous body. He was lean and wiry and, unlike her, had almost no body fat. Straight dark hair short enough to behave and long enough to run her fingers through. And his eyes—bright turquoise, intelligent and serious. She would have paid money to see what his eyes did when he laughed.

Simone's grandmother would have called him a long drink of water. Simone never quite understood what that meant until the moment Jason raised his arm to take a book off the top shelf and Simone saw every single muscle in his long strong back shift under his skin. A long drink of ice-cold water on a hot day. She would drink that glass empty and then lick the sweat off the sides.

Professional, she reminded herself. Stop ogling the models.

"This'll do," Jason said, turning around with a book in his hand. "Thought I ought to pose with a book I like in case someone asks me about it."

He had an old leather-bound hardcopy of Robert Penn Warren's *All the King's Men* in his hand.

"You've read it?" Simone asked.

"I have," he said. She was ashamed of herself for being impressed. She hadn't expected a bull rider, even a retired one, to read novels, much less American classics. Showed what she knew about the price of bourbon in Kentucky.

"What's it about?" Simone asked as she helped move Jason into position. She posed him sideways, leg forward, so that even when he dropped the towel, the camera would just see his side, hip and thighs. Although she'd heard of the book she wasn't dying to read it. All she wanted was to get Jason talking and distracted, to make it easier for him to be naked in front of her.

Simone picked up her camera and placed it to her eye to find the best angle for the shot.

"A man who works for the corrupt governor of Louisiana has to dig up dirty secrets on a judge he respects. Then he finds out more than he wanted to find out about the judge and his own family," Jason said.

"I like family secret books," she said. "Seems like every family has a dark secret."

"Do they?"

"My grandmother had a baby before she was married and gave her up for adoption. She never told anyone. We only found out after she died. Not a very dark secret but it really upset my mother to know she had a sibling out there she'd never met. What about you?"

"If we had a family secret, I wouldn't tell it to anyone."

Simone shook her head and smiled. "I'm just going to shut up now and take the pictures."

"Why?" he asked.

"I keep putting my foot in my mouth around you."

"It's my fault. I'm just out of practice. I've been hanging out with horses for months. Forgotten how to talk to women."

"You're doing fine."

"So are you."

"Good. Ready to take the towel off? It's okay if you aren't. I have all day."

"Might as well get it over with."

"You can drop it right on the floor. I'll be shooting from the thigh up. And the door is locked, so don't worry about anyone walking in on us." Simone turned around to give him some privacy. A few seconds passed.

"Can you help me?" Jason asked.

"Taking your towel off?" she asked, trying not to sound hopeful.

"Not that."

She turned around. He still had his towel on. He seemed to be trying to take off the little gold chain he wore around his neck.

"You got smaller hands than me," he said.

Simone went to him, happy to oblige. She stood behind his back and quickly and easily unclasped the chain. Being that close to him was a heady experience. He smelled like Ivory soap from a recent shower. His nervousness had raised his body temperature. She could feel the heat radiating off of him. Had he been a friend of hers, Griffin maybe, she would have pressed herself against him or slapped his ass to make him laugh. She wasn't sure she'd heard Jason laugh yet. She wondered if he ever did. He really was nothing like the other men she'd photographed for these calendars. The baseball player—Mets catcher—she'd photographed last year had hit on her the entire time, teasing her about how she ought to take him out to dinner before getting him naked. The Broadway star two years ago had regaled her with hilarious backstage gossip the entire time. And the real estate mogul had tried to sell her a condo. Jason was different. So polite. So quiet. Especially for a man who'd won millions of dollars on the professional bull-riding circuit. She'd expected a cocky cowboy, not this quiet, humble, solemn man.

No wonder they called him "Still" Waters.

"Thank you," he said, turning to face her. She held up the necklace.

"Pretty cross," she said. "I'll put it with my things so it doesn't get lost."

She set it carefully inside her camera bag.

"Mom would kill me if she knew I was doing this," Jason said. "She'd kill me twice if I was wearing that in the picture."

"I guess she's pretty religious?" Simone asked.

Jason nodded as he moved back into place.

"Dad, too. Even more than Mom. Well, maybe not more than Mom. But he's...tougher about it."

Jason said "tougher." Simone heard "meaner." She wondered if maybe there was more than milder winters that brought Jason to Kentucky from Montana.

"What about you?" Jason asked as he dropped the towel onto the floor. He didn't wait for her to turn her back again. He seemed over the nervousness now.

"What about me?"

"You got a cross tattooed on your arm."

"Oh," she said, smiling as she raised her camera's

viewfinder to her eye. "That's not for me. My family celebrates Christmas and Hanukkah but we're not all that religious. The cross is ah...long story."

"I like long stories. Takes my mind off being buck naked in the damn library."

Simone got off a couple good shots. Jason was handsome, yes. Strong jaw, straight nose, soulful eyes, which you'd expect on a man who'd regularly faced death for a living. But he was also photogenic, which was different from simply being attractive. Some people took good pictures. Some didn't. Jason did.

"It might offend you," she said.

"Call my horse ugly and you might offend me. Nothing much else is going to do it."

Simone laughed. Jason still didn't. But he smiled. Sort of.

"I'm a part-time photographer," she said. "And a part-time pro-sub."

"What's that?"

"You know what a dominatrix is?"

His brow furrowed. "The lady with the whips and chains and leather boots?"

"That's it," she said. "I'm kind of the opposite of that. Professional dominatrixes top men for money. Pro-submissives submit to men for money. Or women. Although it's almost always men." Simone kept shooting. Jason was doing a very good job of keeping his face impassive while he pretended to read his book, as he said, buck naked in the library. "I had a few very special masters in my career. The cross is a tribute to one of them. He's a very religious man. Very devout Catholic. Even when he was flogging me, he could make it...what's the word? Sacred?"

"Sacred?" Jason asked. "Nice."

Simone nodded, surprised. Surprised and impressed. She didn't think he'd take the news of her other career this well. He really was hard to offend. Rare to find a man who was exactly what he said he was.

"Exactly," she said. "That's the word."

"And you liked him so much you got a tattoo for him?"

"He's a special guy," she said. "And he was very good to me."

"Must have been. I never had a girl so impressed with me that she rolled right out of bed and got my name tattooed on her arm."

Simone laughed. So much for her theory Jason was a sweet, innocent virgin. Although there was something about him, something she couldn't put her finger on. He wasn't a virgin but he was...something. Maybe lonely?

"We never slept together. Pro-subs don't have sex with their masters. It's a different thing. Hard to explain. Certain people, even if you're not lovers or in love or whatever...I don't know, they can leave a mark on you. Can you shift your right leg forward a little bit and your left hip back?"

Jason moved his leg. She could see a little too much Jason Junior in the shot.

"I hope that doesn't freak you out," she said. He didn't seem freaked out. Didn't seem all that fascinated, either. He was just making polite conversation.

"Didn't know that was a job is all," he said.

"In New York it is."

"How you get that job? Hang a shingle?"

Simone grinned at the idea of a little storefront with a hanging shingle sign that read "Simone Levine - Professional Whipping Girl." Her logo could be a picture of a hand spanking a bare ass.

"Not quite," she said. "I know I don't look the part, but I was actually one of those super annoying overachiever kids. Started college at seventeen. Graduated at twenty. Started a PhD program five minutes later mostly to make my parents happy. Masochist, right?"

"Sounds like it."

"I needed a job that could help pay the bills but had flexible enough hours I could still handle school. I'd hung out at this kinky club for a couple years, and I asked the owner if he'd let me go pro. I started working for him the next night. Got more out of the job than I did school. Eventually I quit school and have been doing it ever since."

"So how'd you get to be a photographer?"

She laughed. "Advertising my sub services online," she said. "I could never find anyone to take good fetish pictures of me so I started taking them myself. Turned out I was good at it. Now I'm a part-time pro-submissive and a professional freelance photographer. Between the two I can pay the bills."

"You still do it?" he asked.

"Not as much as I used to. I travel so much now taking pics that I don't get to do it as much as I'd like."

"So you ah...you really do like it?"

"Love it," she said. "It's not for everyone, but it is for me."

Simone got off a few more shots. Sexy as Jason was, she almost wanted to take a couple pictures just for her own private collection. Maybe a nice back shot. The man's back side was nearly as nice as his front side. She didn't take a picture of his ass, but she did commit it to memory.

"That's good," she said. "You can put your towel back on."

Jason wrapped up while she flipped through the pictures she'd taken.

"Good news," she said. "Your shots turned out great. We're done."

"That's it?" he asked.

"That's it. I know. Kind of anti-climactic. All that stress and it's over in ten minutes. But you take great pics. You can get dressed whenever."

Simone started packing her gear as Jason went behind the screen again. When he came out she brought his cross over to him and clasped the chain around his neck. She resisted the urge to hug him. He probably wouldn't have liked that. He didn't seem like a hugger.

She had him sign the release form and he did it without hesitation before passing it back to her.

"It was nice to meet you," she said. "I'll let you get back to your life now. The organizers will be in touch soon."

She held out her hand to shake and he shook it. Good hands, strong and steady.

"Nice to meet you, Miss Simone," he said.

"It was a pleasure working with you, Mister Waters."

He started for the door. Typical shoot. All done. Yet Simone regretted it was over so soon. She almost wished the light had been bad so they would have had more time together.

Jason opened the door but then he closed it again, turned around and leaned back against it.

"What's up?" she asked.

Jason didn't meet her eyes. He took a long breath and held up a hand. He needed a second.

"Regretting it already?" Simone asked. "I can delete the pics right now. Every last one. It's no big deal."

"They paid you to fly to Kentucky. It would be a big deal."

"It's no big deal," she said again. "Just say the word."

"That's not it," he said.

"What's wrong?" Simone crossed her arms over her chest and waited. "Tell me, Jason. Please?"

"You said, ah...you still sometimes, you know, do your other job?" he asked, crushing his hat in his hands again.

"Pro-subbing? Yes? You know someone who needs one?" Simone imagined it wasn't easy to find kink professionals in rural Kentucky.

"Yeah," he said. "Me."

3

As soon as the words were out of his mouth, Jason wanted to snatch them right out of the air and swallow them whole. Simone was staring at him like he'd grown a second head.

What the hell had he been thinking?

"Pretend I didn't say that," he said. "Have a good day, ma'am."

He started to leave right that second but Simone stopped him by running up to him and putting her hand on the doorknob.

"Yes," she said.

"What?"

"Yes. I'm available. If you need a session with a pro, I can do that. Just...don't run out on me before we can talk about it."

"I can't even believe I said that." He shook his head

and looked up at the ceiling, trying to avoid her pretty, worried eyes.

"I won't lie, I'm a little shocked myself," she said. "But not in the bad way. I'm glad you asked. It's okay if you're kinky. I am, too. Very."

"I'm not."

"Not kinky? Usually vanilla men don't ask for sessions with pro-submissives."

"I don't know. Maybe I am. Maybe I'm crazy, too. Wouldn't surprise me."

"I'm not crazy," she said. "Kink and crazy aren't the same thing, I promise. Can we talk about this? Please?"

Her eyes were wide and beseeching. So hard to say no to a pretty girl who said "please" like that.

"I ought to get back to work. I've lost enough of the day," he said.

Jason didn't really want to go to work. He wanted to stay with this wide-eyed, pink-haired, smiling girl who said things he'd never heard anyone say before like "Our bodies are nothing to be ashamed of" and "Kink and crazy aren't the same things."

Hell, if she just kept saying things like that to him all day, he'd pay her every penny he had in the bank.

"We can get coffee. Or I can come over to your place," she said. Her voice was gentle, like his got when he was trying not to spook a skittish horse. He must look spooked. "I'd love to meet Rusty. And we can get to know each other a little better. Then if you want to try a half-hour session or something, we can do that. I'd really like that."

Jason took another long breath. He thought he might pass out. Took a bull horn to the guts and it hadn't rattled him as much as talking about this stuff did.

"I never..." he began and he didn't have to finish.

"First time for everything," she said. "You never took your clothes off for a charity calendar before today, right? And it wasn't that bad, right?"

She gave him that sweet smile again, the one that went all the way to the corners of her eyes. He'd told her the one thing about himself he'd been scared to tell anyone else in the world and she still seemed to like him. That helped.

"I don't think I'll be able to go through with it," he said. "Paying for you to...whatever you do."

"Let's forget about a paid session then," she said. "I'll do what you said and pretend you never brought it up. But we can talk, right? I think we should."

"We should?"

"You have to have questions," she said. "And you must be feeling pretty lonely if you've wanted to do this for a while and never had the chance. People in my—I guess you could call it a 'community'—we try to take care of our own. Like you and your friend Luke, right? You rodeo guys all got each other's backs?"

"We try."

"If you have these feelings, whether you've ever

acted on them or not, you're part of my community. You're one of us. I'd like the chance to have your back," she said. She was still smiling but in a more serious sort of way. She wasn't joking with him. She meant all that and that meant a lot to him.

"I guess talking about it won't kill me," he said, though he wasn't going to bet the farm on that. His heart beat hard in his chest and his stomach flipped over and back again. If he puked once or twice before this day was over he wouldn't be surprised.

"I have my rental car. How about I follow you to your place if it's not too far?"

"Not too far," he said.

"Great. Just give me ten minutes to pack up."

"You need some help?"

"Nah. No offense, but I don't like anyone but me touching my equipment. My photography equipment, that is. Other equipment is negotiable."

He pointed at her. "That's flirting."

"Just trying to make you laugh," she said as she started to take down her weird lighting umbrellas or whatever they were. "Haven't had any luck yet."

"Know any good jokes?" he asked.

"A couple. Mostly Catholic jokes, though. My old boss, Mr. King, he told those all the time."

"I can take a Catholic joke."

"Let's see..." She put her binder in a duffel bag and wrapped up her camera good and tight. "I got it. A priest is driving and a cop pulls him over. The cop smells a little alcohol on the priest's breath. He says to the priest, 'Father, have you been drinking?' The priest says, 'Just water.' The cop asks, 'Then why do I smell wine?' The priest picks up the bottle and says, 'Praise the Lord! He's done it again!'"

Jason groaned but the groan turned into a laugh. A little one.

"Now that's a miracle," Simone said, pointing at Jason's grinning face.

"I heard this one," Jason said. "A priest, a rabbi and a minister walk into a bar. The bartender looks up and says..."

"Is this some kind of joke?" Simone said, already ahead of him with the punch line.

They laughed together. It was a little awkward but good awkward. Kind of nice, too. He hadn't had time to date or anything since he'd moved to Kentucky last year. The farm needed all his attention, Jason had told himself. A good excuse to avoid facing the reasons he'd left Montana.

Then the pink lady here had to walk into his life. He wasn't sure he was one of those sorts who believed in signs, but he couldn't help but feel he was being given a chance here, and he'd be a damned fool if he didn't take it.

Jason watched Simone dismantle her equipment and pack it up neatly. At least she allowed him to carry a couple of the bags down to her rental car so he didn't feel completely useless.

"I'll drive slow," he said. "I'm in that old red Ford over there. Can't miss it."

"I'll be right behind you," she said. "And if you change your mind and speed off, I will follow you no matter where you go. I've always wanted to be in high speed car chase."

"That's a 1987 Ford. It's gonna be a low-speed chase."

"Then me and my Kia will run you down. See you at your farm. And don't worry, for a kinky freak, I'm very nice."

She winked at him and he shut her car door for her. As he pulled out of the parking lot and onto the highway, he watched her carefully in the rearview mirror as she followed him. As nervous as he was about her coming to his farm, he was more nervous she might change her mind and drive off, leaving him high and dry. He couldn't imagine this was going to work out but even if they could talk a little, if she could tell him a few things he didn't know, that would be worth all the stress and humiliation he was feeling and had been feeling for about as long as he could remember.

They came to the turn that led to his horse farm and Jason caught himself holding his breath to make sure she took it behind him. After he turned there was a full thirty-second gap before a break in traffic allowed her to catch up to him. Longest thirty seconds of his life. He put his foot on the gas and drove a steady twenty all the way to his place.

Trees mostly shaded his farmhouse so there was no seeing the place until you'd pulled right into the driveway. He hoped Simone liked his farm. He loved it and had loved it at first sight. He had a sixty-acre spread with two barns, two outbuildings, and four pastures surrounded by wooden fences painted black. The house itself was white, two stories, with a big back deck and red brick chimney on the side. He pulled into the driveway and parked, got out and waited for her.

She was smiling—of course she was—when she stepped out of her car.

"Wow," she said. "This is all yours?" She glanced around her, eyes wide.

"It's not much. Sixty acres, that's all."

"That's all?"

"My folks have a thousand acres back home," he said. "Cattle need more room than horses."

"I live in a 500-square-foot apartment," she said.

"Yours probably cost more than mine," he said.

"I wish you were joking," she said. "Can I meet Rusty?"

"Sure. This way."

They walked down the asphalt path to the first barn. It was a nice day with a blue sky and no clouds, but it wasn't quite warm yet. Jason slipped out of his flannel shirt and draped it over Simone's shoulders.

"Thanks," she said. She'd been hugging her arms to her stomach to warm herself.

"Barn's heated," he said.

"I thought the south was warmer than New York."

"It is. But you're not very far south yet. Hope you didn't pack a swimsuit."

"I wasn't that dumb," she said. "I did pack a miniskirt though. That was a mistake."

"You got good legs?" he asked.

"Pretty decent."

"Not a mistake then."

Simone put her arm through his. He liked that. He liked that a lot. So much he glanced up at the sky to hide the sudden smile he couldn't suppress. Though the day was bright and sunny, he couldn't help but wish a storm would kick up so she'd be stranded at his house for good long time.

"So you train horses here?" she asked.

"I do."

"Train them to do what?"

"Behave," he said. She laughed. "Not kidding. You gotta train them like a dog. They have to learn to trust humans. Then you gotta teach them to take commands. I mostly train horses for barrel racing but we got a couple out here I'm training as therapy horses. A couple more for trail riding. Little bit of everything."

"And you do all that yourself?"

"I don't work with more than six to eight horses at a time."

"Any money in that?"

"I made all the money I'm ever gonna need. I do this for me. When you're a bull rider, it's man *versus* animal. You're enemies. But with horses, you're a team. It's good for me, getting a horse to trust me, to do what I want. They have a mind of their own, you know. They want to do things their way, and I have to train them to do things my way."

"How do you do that?"

"Well, I just show them that when they do things my way, good things happen."

"Hmm..." she said.

"What?"

"Sounds a little like training a submissive."

Jason was about to ask her what she meant by that when his farm manager Franco came out of the barn.

"You're back early," Franco said.

"And I brought a friend. Simone, this is Franco. Franco, Simone."

"Nice to meet you," Franco said. They shook hands.

"*¿Quieres el resto del día libre?*" Jason asked Franco in Spanish. *Do you want the day off?*

"I'll take it if you don't need me. I have to pick some things up in town," Franco said.

"I'll see you tomorrow," Jason said.

In English Franco told Simone goodbye, tipped his hat to her, and headed to his truck.

"Farm manager," Jason explained as they went into the barn.

"Nice guy," she said. "From Mexico?"

"Yeah, we get horse people from two different countries here in Kentucky," he said. "Ireland and Mexico. For some reason I can't quite figure out, it's only the guys from Mexico the politicians raise a fuss about. They never ask the Irish guys for their papers."

"Can't imagine why." She rolled her eyes.

Jason took her to the first stall where Rusty was, face down in his oats.

"Hey, boy," Jason said. "There's a girl here wants to meet you."

Rusty kept right on eating.

"No manners," Jason said to Simone. "I apologize for this heathen."

Simone didn't seem offended. She just patted Rusty's shoulder and mane while the horse kept on chowing down.

"You're different than I expected," Simone said.

"Rusty or me?"

"You," she said. "I guess I expected...I don't know. You didn't bat an eyelash when I mentioned that my friend Griffin had a boyfriend. Didn't blink when I said my family was half-Jewish. You didn't get offended when I said I was a pro-submissive. You speak Spanish well enough to tell your manager he can have the day off."

"So you picked that up."

"New Yorker," she said. "Half my neighborhood is

Puerto Rican. I should apologize for assuming you were some kind of a..."

"Redneck?" he asked.

"I would never ever use that word," she said. "Even if I might have maybe thought it. But I won't admit to that."

"You New York elites," he said, grinning at her so she'd know he was kidding. "Facts are...I got too much to do every day to worry about what two grown men are doing with each other in their bedrooms, and if other people do, they need a hobby or a job. I was raised to respect other people's religions and to mind my own business. I know Spanish because some of the best bull riders in the world are from Mexico, and one of them, Vicente de la Rosa, happens to be my uncle by marriage. As for you being what you are, well, I can't say it doesn't bother me, but that's only because what I am bothers me, too."

Rusty finally raised his head from his bucket.

"Oh, hi there," Simone said, smiling at the big chestnut Quarter Horse. "You finally finish?"

"About time," Jason said. He reached over the stall gate and gave his old boy a firm pat on the side. "I was about to have to take your bucket away. You got to mind your manners when there's a lady present."

"He's a good boy," she said. She seemed enchanted by Rusty. She kept running her small hand over his shoulder and mane.

"So what are you, Jason?" she finally asked.

"Damned if I know," he said.

"You must have some idea," she said. "You have fantasies, right?"

He sighed heavily. The word "fantasies" had made his stomach lurch. "This is not going to be easy to talk about."

"My friend Nora's a switch," Simone said. "Do you know what that is?"

He shook his head.

"She likes to dominate *and* submit. She started out as just a submissive, though. Now she's a dominatrix but she also has a master. She says it took her about ten years to really figure out what she was. And that's pretty normal for a lot of us. But me—she calls me a natural. Said some people are just lucky to get it from day one. The second I learned what kink was, that was the second I knew I was kinky. And as soon as I knew what submission was, I knew that was me. Once I was old enough to do it, I did it. I loved it. I've been doing it ever since. Never lost a wink of sleep over what I do. Kind of sounds like you've lost some sleep over this."

"A little," he said. "A lot maybe."

"Okay," she said, nodding. "Let me list a few things for you. You tell me if any of them sound like something you might be interested in trying."

"All right," he said, bracing himself.

"Spanking, flogging, cropping, caning, dripping hot candle wax onto naked flesh, bondage—rope, cords,

silk scarves, chains—slapping, choking, foot worship...
anything ringing any bells?"

Jason only stared at her for what felt like a year.

"People do that stuff to you?" he asked.

"Yeah," she said. "But only consensually. Why?"

"Maybe I'm not so screwed up after all."

4

Simone glared at him. She knew he'd been making a joke but she didn't want to hear any of that negative talk, even as a joke.

"You," she said, poking him in the chest, "are not screwed up just because you have kinky thoughts. I am not screwed up, either. You have to get that stupid idea out of your head. It's an insult to me, my friends, my world...and an insult to you."

Jason took a deep breath. "Easier said than done."

They left Rusty content in his stall and walked down the length of the barn. Jason brought her to a large sink and together they rolled up their sleeves and washed the horse hair off their hands.

"You're not going to answer my question?" she asked. "None of that worked for you?"

"Some of it, I guess, maybe," he said. He handed her a towel and she dried off.

"Which ones?"

"Let's go in the house. The horses don't need to hear this."

It was a good thing Jason was handsome. Made up a little for how frustrating he was being. A very little.

Simone hoped the walk to the house would get him talking, but he didn't say a single word all the way from the barn, up the path, and to the back door. They went inside and she found herself in his kitchen. It was old-fashioned and charming—white tile, porcelain sink, yellow paint, white curtains, a red rooster cookie jar.

"Cute," she said.

"My sister Aimee came down for a couple of weeks after I moved in," he said. "She stole my credit card and put the whole place together in ten days. Woman's a miracle worker. I'd still be eating off a card table if she hadn't put everything to rights."

Simone sensed he'd mentioned his sister for a reason. "You two close?"

He nodded. "She's my best friend. We're only a year apart. And we have a lot in common. She's a world-champion barrel racer herself. Or used to be before she quit to give me two nieces." He pointed at his refrigerator and a picture of twin girls with brown hair in pigtails.

"What are their names?" Simone asked.

"Dani and Cassie," he said. "That one's Dani." He

pointed at the twin with red ribbons in her hair. "That one's Cassie."

"They're adorable," Simone said with a grin. "Your parents must be proud of you and your sister."

"They are."

"You close to them?" she asked.

"I love them. Mom would do anything for us kids, and Dad's always been a good provider."

"That's not an answer to my question." Simone noticed he was very good at answering questions without answering them.

Jason pointed to the kitchen table, a small round table with yellow legs and matching pale yellow chairs. She sat down and he sat across from her.

"Dad's strict," Jason said. "Old-fashioned. No sparing the rod with him."

"Was he hard on you and your sister?"

Jason sort of frowned and shook his head.

"Just me," he said. "Aimee's the princess, not that she wanted that."

"What do you mean?"

"I remember...Aimee was eleven and I was ten. She and I got into it over something, and she just jumped on my last nerve. I screamed at her. We were upstairs. Dad heard us."

"You screamed at your sister? Shocking. You know that's kind of normal, right?"

"Not in my family it isn't. Men do not raise their

voices to women in my family. It is not done at all. My first word wasn't 'mom.' It was 'ma'am.'"

"You were only ten. You weren't a man. You were a little kid."

"Didn't matter. Dad jerked me out of the house by the arm. Thought he was going to yank it out of the socket. I was behind that woodshed with him for about an hour. Could barely sit for a week. But I think Aimee was more upset about it than I was."

Except it was Jason telling the story with the ghost of a terrified little boy in his eyes. He could pretend that hadn't hurt him, but Simone could see it left scars.

"Your father beat you for raising your voice to your sister? When you were ten? My sister and I had knock-down-drag-out fights. Doesn't every kid do that?"

"Men do not do that in my family," Jason said again. "I only had to look crossways at my sister or mother and it would mean another trip back to the woodshed. And to even think of hitting a woman? If Dad ever thought I'd laid a finger on a girl I wouldn't be allowed under the roof again for the rest of my natural life."

"Is that it? Is that what you fantasize about?" she asked. "Hitting women?" Simone kept her voice low and gentle. She thought they were getting somewhere —finally. "It's okay if you do," she said. "I like being spanked. Lots of women do."

She was trying to tease him into answering, but

from the look of anguish on his face, she realized this wasn't a confession she could tease out of him. Jason rubbed his forehead with his right hand, his elbow polishing the table top. He dug his hand into his hair and Simone saw his eyes were rimmed in red.

"Jason?" Simone said. "You can tell me. Do you fantasize about hitting women?"

Slowly, very slowly, he nodded.

She stood up and patted the air to tell him to stay seated. She stood in front of his kitchen chair and took his face in her hands.

"That wasn't so bad, was it?" she asked.

"I can't believe I told you that."

"I'm glad you told me. You ever tell anyone else?"

He shook his head.

"Does anyone know?" she asked.

Jason didn't answer at first so Simone knew someone must know. Without asking for permission—easier to ask forgiveness, anyway—she sat on Jason's lap and wrapped her arms around his shoulders. He didn't complain or ask what she was doing. He simply put his arms around her waist to keep her from falling off his lap.

She tapped her chest twice, over her heart and Jason rested his forehead there against her skin.

"It's easier to talk like this sometimes," she said. "Close contact but no eye contact."

"Aimee," he said.

"Your sister knows?"

"She borrowed my laptop without asking me first."

"She saw something?"

Jason nodded.

"Kinky stuff?" she asked.

"Porn," he said. "A girl tied up and getting hit with some kind of whip. It freaked her out."

Simone winced. She'd seen some porn online that had even freaked *her* out. "Was this before or after you moved here?"

"Before. Right before."

"Was she mad at you?" Simone asked.

"She said I ought to get some help."

"Good advice. Now you're getting help. From me."

"Not sure that was what she meant."

"Doesn't matter. If she's not kinky she doesn't know what kind of help you need. I do."

"You do?"

"I absolutely do," Simone said. "But you're going to have to tell me a little more so I know what we're working with here. There's a big difference between wanting to spank a woman with her permission and wanting to punch a woman in the face without it. Can you tell me which of those is more your style?"

"I'd never hit a woman," Jason said. "I mean, not... like that. I don't even know if I'd like doing it. I just, it's what works for me up here." He tapped his forehead.

"You have kinky fantasies when you masturbate?"

He groaned softly.

"Jason, everybody does it. I do. I did this morning, in fact," she said with pride. "Big hotel bed. Plenty of room to wiggle around."

"Nice thought," he said, smiling.

"I like the image of you stroking yourself off, too," she said. "It's very sexy."

"It is?"

"You could tie me down and come on me," she said. "That would be fun."

He groaned again. It was a much nicer groan that time.

"Thought you said you didn't do that with your clients," he said.

"I don't want you to be a client," she said. "Too many walls and rules. I'd rather we just keep getting to know each other, and then we'll see what happens."

Simone knew she was taking a risk here, but she liked Jason so much already. She sensed he needed more help than a pro could give him. What he needed was a friend he could really confide in and trust. He needed her.

"I've known you all of two hours," he said. "I can't believe I'm telling you this stuff about me."

"Easier to tell a stranger," she said. "It's why people go to priests for confession. And you can confess to me. Anything. Anything at all. Trust me, I've either heard it before or heard worse."

"I hear it in my head," he said, "and it sounds so

awful to me. Too awful to say out loud. Especially to a girl."

"Jason, I had a client once who tied me to a chair and spent the next hour describing in gruesome detail how much it would turn him on to kill me, cut me into little pieces, cook me, and eat me. Literally eat me. Not the sexy way of eating girls. He wanted me on a plate. I was a vegetarian for two weeks after that. Is what you want going to be more awful than that?"

She felt Jason's shoulders moving under her hands.

"Are you puking or laughing?" she asked. "I can't tell."

"I don't know," he said. "Both?"

"At least that guy tipped well. He invited me to dinner after the session. I took the money. I declined the dinner invite."

"Smart girl."

Simone took a long breath. She wondered how her friend Mistress Nora did this all the time with her clients—got them to trust her, talk to her, confide in her. If Nora were here she'd know what to do or say to Jason to make him open up.

"I knew some submissive men who really struggled with their kinks," she said. "Never known a dominant man to have this much trouble talking about it."

"I don't feel all that dominant."

"Do you want to feel dominant?" she asked. "Is that it?"

"I want to," he said. "In my head I am. In my head

it's easy. Now that you're here and you're willing, I hope—"

"Very, *very* willing."

"I just can't...I can't talk about it."

"Is it that bad?" she asked. "Do you have, I don't know, rape fantasies? It's okay if you do. My boss and his lady did rape-play. I've never done it, but I'm trained for it."

"It's like that. Worse maybe."

"Is it something you think is kind of gross? Like scat play?"

"God, no."

"Whew." Simone laughed and waited for Jason to laugh with her. He didn't. "Can you tell me why you're having so much trouble with this?"

Jason slowly lifted his head and met her eyes.

"I need to believe I'm a good man," he said. "I don't know if I can be *that* or do *that* and also be a good man."

Simone held out her arm to display her tattoo of the cross.

"He's a good man," she said, pointing to the cross tattoo. "And he's a sadist. A real one. The kind who can only get turned on when he's inflicting pain. He was good, though, because he never inflicted pain on women who didn't want that pain. It was mutual. It was fun. He would take my face in his hands before we played, look deep in my eyes, and tell me how much he appreciated my service to him. Then he'd flog me and cane me and whip me into another dimension of reality. Afterwards, he'd do this with me—sit me on his lap and just hold me while I came back down to earth. And then he'd tell me how much better he felt, all thanks to me. He meant it, too. It always made me feel so special. He never even kissed me, except on the forehead. But I felt closer to him than people I'd slept with."

"Service," Jason said. "I like that word."

"Is that what you're into? You want a woman to serve you?"

"In my mind..."

"In your sexual fantasies, you mean?"

Jason nodded. "In there, it's more than that."

"Like...what? Sexual slavery?" Simone asked.

"Kind of. Maybe. That's bad, right?"

Simone's heart danced in her chest. She knew they were getting closer to a breakthrough.

"Real slavery is bad, obviously," she said. "But we're not talking about the real deal. I mean, out there, outside your door, in the real world, slavery is pure evil. But in here, where it's just you and me, it's not the real world. It's *our* world. And it doesn't have to be bad if we don't want it to be bad. It could be our own private fun thing."

"Fun? If I made you my slave, you would find that fun?" Jason sounded skeptical.

"With you, I think it could be," she said.

"You wouldn't be scared to do something like that?"

"Not as long as you promise to honor my safe word."

"What is it?"

"Jellybean."

He raised his head, eyebrow cocked high. "Jellybean? Seriously?"

"My hair used to be rainbow-striped. A friend said it looked like jellybean colors so he called me Jellybean as a joke."

"Cute. I like the pink, though."

"Thank you," she said, grinning with pleasure. Not every day a sexy cowboy told her he liked her pink hair. "I know you know how safe words work. As long as you don't hear me saying 'jellybean' you know I'm into what we're doing. So you can keep doing it. And doing it. And doing it..."

"There's so much I'd like to do to you, with you."

"Tell me, Jason. Please?"

"I'd give you orders, make you serve me."

"What kind of orders? Make the bed? Sweep the floors? Change light bulbs naked?"

"Suck me," he said. "On your knees. Let me fuck you whenever I wanted, however I wanted, whether you were in the mood or not. And if you didn't do what I wanted you to do just the way I wanted you to do it..."

"You'd punish me?"

"Yeah."

"By spanking me or cropping me?"

"Right."

Jason was breathless now, and so was she. She couldn't imagine how difficult it was for Jason to admit all this to her. For a man—raised by a father who beat him just for raising his voice to his sister—to confess to having fantasies about keeping a woman as a slave... she didn't know whether to pat him on the back or kiss him. She did neither. His eyes were technicolor blue, hooded and glassy, like he'd ingested some potent cocktail, and she could tell he was hard. She could feel it through her jeans. And he'd pulled her closer to him. Not close enough. Until he was all the way inside her, it wouldn't be close enough. The world had shrunk down to the size of Jason's kitchen. There was no one on the planet but the two of them. She wouldn't break the spell for all the money in the world.

"Bad behavior should be punished," she said. "I mean, otherwise how would I learn how to behave?"

"No other way," he said.

"None I can think of," she said. "And if a girl like me was owned by a man like you and I didn't serve you the way you ought to be served, then I'd probably deserve to be punished."

Ah, she loved this game so much.

"But not too rough," he said. "I wouldn't want to hurt you or break your spirit." He ran his hand through her hair, spun one little curl around his finger. "Just teach you, train you."

"Train me to be your perfect slave?"

"No such thing as perfect. Always room for improvement."

"I would love to learn how to serve you," she said softly into his ear. "A man like you should have a girl of your own to use when you need her. When a man like you needs his cock sucked, he shouldn't have to wait for it. If you had your own little slave, you wouldn't have to wait." She punctuated her little speech with a kiss on his ear. He shivered.

"Nobody wants to wait for what they need," he said. "Not that I'd be cruel to you. If I owned a girl like you, I'd take real good care of you."

"To be owned by a man like you would be an honor for a girl like me. Even if it was only for a night."

"You think we could try?" he asked, sounding equal parts scared and hopeful.

"I'd love to try it with you," she said. "I'd love to serve you all night."

He smiled a little. "You're only saying that because it's your job."

"I'm not charging you a cent," she said. "I want this."

"You mean it?"

"I'm wet, Jason. That's how you know I mean it."

"Are you?"

"I swear," she said. Simone touched his cheek and looked into his eyes. She'd never wanted to serve a man so much in her life, if only to show him how sexy, fun, and beautiful it could be. Someone needed to show him that. That someone needed to be her.

"All right then," Jason said. "Show me."

"Is that an order?" she asked.

"It's an order."

5

Jason put his hands around Simone's waist and stood her in front of him. Some sort of trance had come over him. His hands weren't even shaking as he unbuttoned Simone's jeans and pushed them slowly down her legs.

He wasn't too surprised to find she wore pink lacy thong panties under her ripped and faded jeans. They were so frilly and feminine and looked so pretty on her full hips that he dipped his head and kissed the little bow at the center. She liked that. He could tell from the way she breathed in when his lips met her skin. If she were his all the time, day and night, he'd make sure she always wore little frilly things under her regular clothes, for his eyes only. He stayed close to her body as he slid her jeans all the way down her calves. He tapped her ankles to signal for her to step out of them. Her panties were so pretty he didn't want to take them off of her yet. Instead he stood up and turned her toward the kitchen table.

"Bend over," he said. She did immediately, obeying the order like she'd been waiting for it.

Jason knew he'd never seen anything in the world to rival the sight of a girl wearing his flannel shirt and pink thong panties bent over his kitchen table. Standing behind her, he put his hand flat on the nicest ass he'd seen in his twenty-nine years and pinched it. He didn't pinch hard, not at first. He still couldn't quite believe he was doing all this without her saying a word to stop him. He pinched her harder, hard enough to leave a red mark behind on her pale skin. She flinched but didn't say a word.

"Spread your legs wide," he said.

Gracefully, she lifted her right foot and, with her toe pointed like a ballerina, placed it onto the floor, leaving a good foot and a half between her ankles. Without waiting for his order, she arched her back, which lifted her hips. An invitation. He accepted it. He hooked his finger under the edge of her thong and slid it down, down, over the curve of her soft ass and down to her pussy, which was bare of hair and warm against his knuckles. He pushed the crotch of her panties over to the side. She was pink here, too, pink and red and wet enough he could see it shimmer. He spread her wider with his fingers, spread her wide enough he was worried he might be hurting her. She groaned a little, but it didn't seem to be a groan of pain.

"Pretty pussy. Pretty ass," he said and couldn't believe those words came out of the same mouth that sang hymns every Sunday morning at the First Presbyterian Church.

Simone said nothing and he wondered if he'd gone too far.

"You don't say thank you when a man pays you a compliment like that?" he asked.

"I'll say anything you tell me to, sir," she said. Her voice was small and girlish, almost timid and sweet as pie.

Sir.

Jason closed his eyes and let that word wash all over him like healing water. "Sir?" he repeated.

"Would you prefer I call you Master Jason?" she asked.

Would he? He might, but he might also faint if she did. He was so hard already that if she got him any harder he'd pass out from loss of blood in the brain.

"Sir is just fine," he said. "Now I want you to say thank you when I pay you a compliment."

"Thank you, sir," she said. He could tell she meant it.

"Good girl."

He wanted to go inside her and he wanted to do it without asking permission first. He wanted to stick his fingers in her like he had every right to do it, like he was a man walking into a house he'd paid for in cash. She had said he could, and there was only one way to find out if she meant it. Jason pushed three fingers into her vagina. He went in slow but not too slow. He pressed firmly, purposefully, and all the way up to the knuckles. Simone's pussy clenched around his fingers but not to push him out. She didn't say her safe word. Instead she moaned a long, low "fuck..."

"I don't like language like that from my girl," he said. "That's not how ladies talk."

"I'm sorry, sir," she said, breathless.

"I'm gonna have to punish you for that. Just so you'll remember for next time."

"Yes, sir," she said.

Jason pulled his fingers out of her and the way she groaned, he wondered if that was punishment enough. Maybe for her, but not for him. He stood to the side of her hip and lifted his hand, ready to swat her ass. He stopped, hand a foot from her flesh. This was it. First time in his life he ever raised his hand to strike a woman. A wave of dizziness hit him. He felt momentarily sick to his stomach. Then Simone spoke again, in her sweet, tender voice.

"I deserve it," she said. "And I want to learn to be better."

She must have sensed his hesitation, sensed the reason for it.

"There's two ways to do things," he said. "My way and your way. We're going to do things my way. You understand?"

"Yes, sir."

He raised his hand higher, two feet from her flesh. She arched her back again, lifting her hips once more. Another invitation. Once more, he accepted it. He slapped her hard, a sharp slap, right on the center of her left cheek. It made a loud quick sound, almost like a pop, and when he looked down at her, he saw the red outline of his hand on her skin. It looked so sexy on her, that handprint, that he gave her one on the right cheek, as well.

After, Jason had to stop and take a few deep breaths to calm himself down.

"Now that wasn't so bad, was it?" he asked, asking himself and her at the same time.

"No, sir."

Jason allowed himself a few more breaths to settle down. He felt drunk, stoned, manic and high and all at the same time. He needed to get control of himself and fast. He had a girl to take care of and he couldn't take care of her if he wasn't in complete control of himself.

"Stand up," he said. Simone stood. He took her by the waist and turned her to face him. They were hip to hip and chest to chest but not eye to eye. She kept her eyes lowered, out of respect.

"You're gonna do a couple things for me right now," he said. She nodded, agreeing before he'd even told her what to do. "You're gonna go out that door over there and through the living room. You'll go up the stairs. At the top of the stairs there's a bathroom and two bedrooms. I want you in the blue bedroom. When you get up there, you're going to turn the bed down, nice and neat. Understand?"

"Nice and neat," she repeated. "Yes, sir."

"There's a rug on the floor. I want you to kneel on it with your back to the door and wait for me. It'll be a few minutes, but I'll be there real soon. Go on now." He snapped his fingers and pointed.

Without another word she padded from the kitchen in her white socks and out the door he'd shown her. He heard her on the steps, going quick, which made him grin. When he gave an order, she hopped to it.

Jason sat down at the kitchen table and stared at the floor where Simone's jeans laid in a pile at his feet. Proof. Proof this was really happening. He put his elbows on the table and rested his face in the cradle of his hands. He inhaled the scent of Simone's body on his fingers. He'd done it. He'd hit a girl with his own hands and the world hadn't ended. He looked for his guilt, his shame, couldn't find it anywhere. That was nice. It had run off and hid for the day. He knew he'd see it again before long but for now, he'd enjoy his time without it.

After one more deep breath, Jason stood up. He felt calm but excited, like he always felt before a ride. He might have ridden eighteen-hundred-pound bulls but nothing had scared him quite like taking those steps upstairs to the guest room where he'd sent Simone. He looked through the door and saw she'd done everything he'd ordered. The bed was neatly turned back, she knelt on the floor, and she wore just her underwear and his shirt, which she'd knotted under her breasts. He left her on the floor waiting while he went into his bedroom and found the box of condoms under his bathroom sink. That wasn't all he wanted, though. In his closet, way in the back corner, he found a riding crop he'd bought at a horse tack store in California, one of the fancy ones that sold dressage and show-jumping equipment. He'd been drawn to the crop at first sight. A jumping bat, it was called. Shorter than a regular riding crop with a wide flapper at the end, big as his palm and smooth brown leather. The lady had asked him if he trained show horses, and he'd lied and said he did.

He returned to the guest room and found Simone still there on the floor, kneeling like he'd ordered. He walked around her, studying her face. Her eyes were lowered again and the expression she wore was one of complete peace. No fear. Not even nervousness. Her confidence gave him confidence.

He pulled off his t-shirt and dropped it on the floor.

Jason extended the crop and put the leather flapper under her chin, lifting it. He'd done that a thousand times in a thousand fantasies but this was the first time he'd ever done it to a real person in real life. His head swam. He swallowed hard before he could speak.

"You're a good little slave," he said softly.

"Thank you, sir," she whispered.

"I haven't kissed you yet. I keep thinking I ought to do that."

"My body's yours, sir," she said. "Every part of it."

"Do you want me to kiss you?" he asked.

"I want what you want, sir."

"I want you to tell me if you want me to kiss you."

"Yes, sir. I would love it if you kissed me."

"If you're a good girl for me, maybe you'll earn a kiss or two."

He'd said that a thousand times in his fantasies. *Earn it. Do it. Obey me. Lay there. Spread for me. Take it. Take all of it...*

But even in his wildest fantasies he never dreamed he'd meet a girl who wanted to hear those words as much as he wanted to say them.

He lowered the crop to his side and stepped forward, right in front of her.

"Take my cock out," he said to her, another line from a thousand fantasies. "Suck it."

She didn't hesitate one second before lifting her hands to unbutton his jeans, to push the denim open and aside to get to him. She wrapped both her small hands around him as she brought the tip to her lips.

"Take it," he said. "Right now. Every inch."

She obliged him with a smile, drawing his cock into her mouth, into her throat. The wet heat of her tongue was heaven. He hadn't had sex in a couple months, and the most recent time had been awkward and disappointing for the both of them. But this was everything he'd wanted for as long as he could remember wanting this. Jason slipped the crop's strap over his wrist and cupped the back of Simone's head in his hands. Gently he moved his hips, fucking her mouth as she sucked him and stroked him. Jason could barely contain himself as she pulled him into her mouth over and over again, rubbed him and pleasured him. Everything was so tight inside him. Every muscle was tense and every nerve vibrated. He could come at any moment.

"Slow down," he said softly and she let up on the intensity. "That's good. I'm going to come on you. When I tap you with the crop, you're going to sit back and open your shirt." She managed somehow to both nod in agreement and keep sucking him at the same time. God, she was good at this.

Jason took his crop in hand again. Now that he wasn't trying to hold off coming, he let himself gaze down at her, watch her. He committed the images to memory—her pink lips wrapped around his cock, her eyes closed in concentration, her bare feet against the rug, his hands twined in her soft hair. He looked up and caught a glimpse of them in the mirror that hung on the back of the door. Simone on her knees with his cock in her mouth and him standing, looming over her with a crop in his hand. Was that him? Really him? The sort of man who did this to women? Made one serve him sexually like a slave? Apparently so. The mirror didn't lie.

The pressure built so hard Jason had to close his

eyes. A groan escaped his throat. His hips moved of their own accord. He needed to come. He'd die if he didn't. He struck the side of Simone's thigh with the crop and she immediately pulled back and with both hands untied the knot and let the shirt fall open. She had beautiful large breasts and red nipples. He came at the sight of them, at the sight of her arching her back, offering herself to him. With his cock in his hand, he came on her chest, on her breasts and stomach and neck in heady, hard spurts. Soft sounds escaped his lips. The pleasure was as intense as he'd ever felt it.

He could barely stand when he'd finished, he was so spent. With his crop he motioned for Simone to lie on the bed. She stretched out on her back and he straddled her hips. He gathered both of her wrists in one hand and pressed them over her head into the sheets. When she was pinned there, covered in his come, looking like every dream he'd ever had in his entire adult life, he finally kissed her.

6

Simone shivered with need and anticipation as Jason straddled her stomach and leaned in to kiss her.

He'd put his fingers inside her pussy, spanked her, and she'd sucked him until he'd come all over her. And yet, they hadn't kissed yet. Not once.

The kiss was more arousing to Simone than if he'd just spent an hour spanking her or fingering her. Her clients never kissed her on the mouth, and she'd been so busy with work, she hadn't been kissed in a long time. Jason looked so sexy looming over her, his strong hand holding her down on the bed. She panted with excitement and Jason gazed at her come-covered breasts as they rose and fell with her every breath.

She'd pleased him. She knew it. And she took enormous pride in that knowledge. She could hardly stop smiling enough to kiss him back when his lips finally met hers. Then he slipped his tongue into her mouth and that was the end of the smiling. The kiss was rough and possessive. He bit her bottom lip and thrust his tongue back into her mouth to make sure she understood he was completely in control of her body.

She understood perfectly.

Simone moaned as he fucked her mouth with his tongue. Years of Jason's pent-up need to dominate came out all at once. She was so glad she got to be his very first. She already wanted to be his second and his third and his...

Jason pulled back from the kiss and looked down at her body again.

"I marked you," he said.

He laid his hand flat on her stomach and slowly massaged his semen into her skin. He rubbed it into her chest and then finally, her breasts. His hand was large and warm and rough on her skin. He cupped her breasts, held them, squeezed them, massaged his come into her until the mark of him was deep in her, deeper than her skin.

"What's going on in that pretty little head of yours?" Jason asked as he continued to rub her breasts. He pinched her nipples lightly, then harder, then harder than that.

"I was um...thinking about photographs," she said.

"Really? Should I punish you for that? I think you should be thinking about me, just me."

"I mean, I was thinking about you and photographs," she said quickly, not that she minded being punished, not at all, not the way Jason did it. "I'm a professional photographer so I put this thing on my pictures so people will know they belong to me. It's called a water-mark. I was just thinking about you marking me like that. Different kind of mark. Same principle. Sir."

"You're marking me, too," he said, the mask of the stern dominant slipping for a moment to reveal the brave yet scared man behind it.

And as the mask slipped so did his grip on her wrists. Simone wriggled her hand free and reached up to touch his face.

That was a mistake.

Jason grabbed her wrist again and pushed it hard into the bed. "Did I tell you could do that?" he asked.

"No, sir."

"Then why did you do it?"

"You're handsome," she said. "Sir."

He narrowed his eyes at her, and she could tell it was killing him not to laugh at her feeble excuse for such a terrible act of disobedience.

"You're going to be punished for that," he said.

Oh, no.

"I'm sorry, sir."

"Sorry's good," he said. "But sometimes sorry's not enough. You understand that, don't you?"

She nodded, biting her bottom lip in mostly

feigned nervousness. This was the most fun she'd had submitting to someone in a long time.

"I'm going to turn you over my knee," he said. "But only because it's how you learn to behave."

He let her up but only so she could roll over and lie across his thighs. Jason brought his hand down hard and the sound of the smack on her ass reverberated through the entire room, as did the sound of her gasp of pain.

The man had one hell of an arm.

He struck her a dozen more times, good hard strikes. The man could spank like he was born for the job *and* had on-the-job training. And when he'd tired of spanking her, he used the crop on her next. Four quick hits right on the reddest, most tender spot. She actually cried out in pain, genuine pain. And the sound of her sudden squeal shocked her so much she laughed.

"I'm sorry, sir," she said quickly, before he could demand the reason for her laughter. Her only response would be "temporary hysteria."

"For what? Laughing?" he asked.

"Yes, sir."

"You think I don't like your laugh?"

"I didn't want you to think I was laughing at you, sir. I was laughing at how hard I screamed."

"I know you were," he said. His voice was smooth and steady and in charge. "You think I don't want a happy slave in my bed? If you're not happy serving me, then it's me doing something wrong, not you."

"You're doing everything right then, sir."

"Am I?"

"You are, sir," she said. "Because I'm very, *very* happy."

Her smile widened as Jason dipped his head and kissed that burning red spot his hand and crop had left on her ass. Or butt. She wasn't sure if she was allowed to say ass. Maybe she'd say it anyway just to find out. She might get another spanking if she did, though.

Oh, the horror. Not that.

"Turn over," he said. Simone obliged. She winced as her sore skin hit his sheets. "You just lie there and rest. I'll be back soon."

"Yes, sir." She wanted to ask him where he was going but she kept her obedient little mouth shut.

Jason returned a couple minutes later with two bottles of water in his hands. He set them on the night-stand and rejoined her in bed.

"Sit up," he said. She sat up. "Here. I don't want you getting thirsty."

He gave her the bottle of water and she drank deeply. She'd done a lot of panting and cock-sucking in the last half hour. She needed that water more than she'd realized. But he'd realized it.

"Thank you, sir," she said. "You take good care of your property."

"You feeling all right?" he asked.

"Wonderful." She grinned at him.

"Are you? You aren't just saying that?"

Simone shifted sideways on the bed to face him where he sat with his back against the headboard.

"This is me," she said. "This is who I am. Sir."

"Are you really a slave?"

"I could be," she said. "For the right master."

"All day and all night?" he said. "Always on duty?"

She nodded. "I think I could. I've dreamed about it."

"You have?"

"Of course," she said. "You've had dreams about it, right? Are you really surprised I have, too?"

"It seems much more fun doing what I do," he said.

"Well, that's because some people are the spankers...and some are the spankees."

Jason laughed a big sexy laugh, so big it shook the bed. "A spankee?" he said, still laughing.

"Exactly. I'm a spankee. You're a spanker."

"That's what I'm calling you from now on," he said. "Spanky. My little rascal."

"Oh, God."

"Is that how you talk to me?" he asked. His brow furrowed and he looked about as mean and dangerous as a little boy glaring at a naughty puppy.

"Oh, God, sir?"

"Better," he said as he reached for her and pulled her to him. "Much better."

He took her by the hips and had her sit across his

thighs. He put his hand in her hair and tilted her head back, her chin up, and he kissed her deep and hard. He was a good kisser. Too good, maybe. When he kissed her, Simone almost forgot she had a flight she had to catch that night.

Jason put his hand on her neck as they kissed, lightly pressing her throat, not hard enough to choke her by any means, but hard enough to remind her he was there and he was in charge.

"I'm going to fuck you," he said against her lips. She said nothing in reply. No reason to. He was going to fuck her. Why argue with the facts?

He lifted her off his lap and pushed her down onto her back again. She lay there, putting up no resistance at all as he slipped her panties off her legs. She thought he'd toss them aside to join his t-shirt on the floor but he didn't.

"I'm keeping these," he said. To show he meant it, he wrapped her pink thong around his wrist, doubling it up like a wrist cuff. It was equal parts sexy, adorable, silly, and possessive, and she adored him for doing it.

She watched as he unzipped his jeans again and lowered them to his thighs, watched as he knelt between her wide open legs and rolled a condom on. He took her by the knees and yanked her a few inches down the bed. He pressed the tip of his cock against her opening and rose up again, entering her fully and with one hard stroke. She sighed and groaned at the penetration. It was rough and deep, deep enough she felt him against her cervix. He took her ankles in his hands and set them on his shoulders. Once she was right where he wanted her to be, he started fucking her with slow, steady thrusts. He'd already come once and didn't seem to be in any hurry to come again. Simone hadn't come yet, and she was about to lose her mind if she didn't. He felt so good inside her. She wanted to close her eyes, concentrate, and come so hard her vagina broke. She found if she turned her head slightly to the right she could watch them fucking in the mirror on the back of the door. He looked so strong, so powerful, so manly and virile as he moved his hips in rough and steady thrusts. She could even see his cock sliding in and out of her. He had one arm wrapped around her thighs to hold her legs in place. Every thrust set nerves deep in her body firing wildly. Shivers danced up and down her spine. In the mirror she saw Jason looking down at her, at their joined bodies. She turned her head again and for a brief moment their eyes met, right before he pumped his cock into her so hard her head fell back against the bed.

Simone moaned as Jason lowered her legs off his shoulders and wrapped them around his back as he crawled on top of her. She flinched in pleasure as he shifted inside her.

"You like it when I use your pussy, don't you?" Jason said.

"Yes, sir."

"You need your pussy used hard, don't you?" he asked.

"Yes, sir," she said. "By you."

"Only me."

"Only you."

The words were dirty pillow talk, the sort of heady, hot-blooded things new lovers said to each other as hormones coursed through their veins and temporarily silenced the rational parts of the brain. But Simone knew if she wasn't careful with this man, she might start to mean some of this stuff.

Jason lowered his head and took her right nipple into his mouth. He sucked it, licked it, sucked it harder, licked it harder and finally nipped it gently with his teeth. The pleasure and the pain mixed and mingled inside her body as he did it all again to her left breast. She clutched the sheets tightly in her fingers as her hips ground wildly up and against his cock.

"You're going to come for me," Jason said as he kissed the valley between her breasts. "Aren't you?"

"Yes, sir."

"But not yet. Not just yet." Jason grasped the shirt she wore—his shirt—and roughly yanked it off her arms. He knelt, still inside her, and Simone watched as he quickly, deftly spun his shirt into a thick rope. Except it wasn't a rope he'd made, but a blindfold. He laid it across her eyes even as he still held onto the two ends. With his hands next to her head, he started to thrust into her again, rough and fast. Simone arched and moaned. He pounded her—there was no other word for it. He pounded her like he owned her.

Simone's clitoris throbbed as his cock rubbed against it with every thrust. She could hardly keep up with the speed of his wild rutting. Finally she let go, surrendered entirely, lying there splayed open on the bed, pinned down and penetrated and split apart. The orgasm was bliss, pure bliss. She came hard, hard enough Jason must have felt it because she heard him gasp as her pussy clamped down onto his cock.

His thrusts continued as she rode out her orgasm. The bed shifted and squeaked under them. This was intense fucking. She could tell from Jason's rapid breathing he was nearly there as well. She lifted her knees and spread her legs as wide as she could, making her body an offering. He accepted the offering and pounded into her one last time before coming with a soft cry that broke her heart for the sweetness of the sound. She had given him pleasure and nothing could please her more than that.

When it was done and over, Jason carefully pulled out of her. She lay on the bed, spent and listless, her eyes still hidden behind his shirt. He'd stolen her panties but if he wasn't careful, she'd steal this shirt. It smelled of his body and their lovemaking. She might never wash it.

Jason left the room, and she knew he'd gone to flush their condom. When he came back a moment later he gently took the shirt off her face and gazed down into her eyes.

"When's your flight tomorrow?" he asked.

"Tonight," she said. "Nine o'five to Newark."

"You're going to change it."

Ah, here it was, the moment the sexy fantasy of being his slave met the reality of real-world commitments. But she didn't really have to be back until Friday when she was booked to photograph a wedding in the Hamptons. Still, just because she could stay four more days didn't mean she should stay four more days. A lot could happen in four days. She could fall in love in four days. She could get her heart broken in four days. But she could also help Jason figure out who and what he was in four days, too. She should stay, for his sake. Right?

Simone smiled up at him.

"Yes, sir."

7

This little scene had never been a part of Jason's fantasies. Simone stood next to him at his kitchen sink, wearing nothing but his shirt. They washed the dishes. Well, she washed. He dried.

In his mind he'd never gotten much further past the visions of a submissive beautiful woman kneeling in front of him or bent over his knee for a spanking or cropping. He really should have added the half-naked girl doing his dishes to the fantasy.

"You just can't do it, can you?" Simone asked him, a little smile on her lips.

"Do what?"

"Sit and watch while a woman does your dishes for you? You have to help?"

"You don't want me to help?" he asked.

"I like the help," she said in that sweet little voice of

hers. "But you cooked dinner. Only fair I do the dishes."

"Spaghetti and toast isn't that hard to cook," he said.

"What's the point of having your own personal slave if you don't let her, you know, slave in the kitchen for you?"

Jason laughed softly. She asked a fair question.

"I'd be a dead man standing here if I ever got it in my head to sit and let a woman in my house wait on me hand and foot. Nothing infuriates Dad more than men being lazy while women work. If Mom or Aimee were working, so were we. Men don't sit while women are still standing. House rules."

"He sounds like a very interesting guy, your dad," Simone said as she passed him a clean wet plate to dry.

"He's a good man," Jason said. "Just not always easy to get along with." Jason put the plate in the cabinet. "I keep thinking how disappointed he'd be in me if he knew about..." Jason sighed. "All this."

"None of his business," Simone said.

"His kids are his business."

"His kids are adults," Simone said. "Once you're out of the house and paying your own bills, it's none of his business." She passed him another plate. "For the record, I'm not disappointed in you. I'm pleased as punch."

He smiled to himself. "You liked all that, did you?"

"You know I did. *Sir.*"

She blushed a little and he nearly threw her down on the kitchen table and had her again just at the sight of that blush.

"I'm not fishing for compliments," he said. "I've never done anything like this before. Had no idea what I was doing up there."

He felt weak admitting all that but it wasn't like Simone didn't already know he was new at this.

Simone shut off the water and dried her hands. She turned around and met his eyes.

"I canceled my flight and rebooked it for Thursday. You really think I'd do that if I wasn't enjoying this with you?"

He smiled. "I'm glad to hear it," he said. "But I...can I ask you something?"

"Of course," she said. They'd finished all the dishes but Jason was in no hurry to leave the kitchen. He liked the sight of her in his shirt standing with her back to the sink. "Ask me anything."

"Am I doing this right?"

"Doing what?"

He shrugged. "This? The master/slave whatever this is?"

"Does it not feel right to you?"

"You know that saying—'This ain't my first rodeo'?" he asked.

"Of course," she said.

"This *is* my first rodeo," Jason said. Simone

laughed. "No, I mean it. I got no idea what I'm doing. So you tell me."

"I'm a pro-sub," Simone said. "I submit for an hour or two here and there to men who pay me. I know how to do a lot of kink, and I enjoy a lot of kink. I've dated kinky people and slept with kinky people, but I've never been the real slave of someone I was in a relationship with. I mean, not that you and I are in a relationship. I just...I mean, you're not paying me."

"Not enough money in the world to pay you for what you're giving me."

"This is what I think," she said. "If you're enjoying it and I'm enjoying it, then we're doing it right."

"I'm not enjoying it," Jason said. "I'm loving every second of it."

She walked over to him where he stood with his back to the counter. She put her hands on his shoulders and looked up into his eyes.

"What?" he asked.

"I was hoping if I stood within kissing distance, you'd kiss me," she said. "You say something like that to a girl, and she'll probably want to be kissed after."

"Is that so?"

"It's so."

"Well, then," he said. He pulled her to him and kissed her. He had a feeling he'd never get tired of kissing this girl. She knew exactly how to let a man lead in a kiss and all the right sounds to make him feel like a man. He lingered over her lips a good long time and when the kiss ended he couldn't bring himself to let her go. He held her to him, arms wrapped around her back, her head against his chest right where it belonged.

"I never got this far in the fantasy," he said. "I should've thought a little farther past the bedroom. You're supposed to be my little slave and I'm supposed to be your big bad master. And yet I can't even let you do my dishes for me. But I can't see myself ordering you around every minute of the day, either."

"There's all different sorts of ways to be a master," Simone said. "I've known nice ones and mean ones and silly ones and sexy ones. Ones who do it an hour or two a week and the ones who do it 24/7 because they can't get off any other way..."

"So you don't have to do it all the time?" Jason asked.

"My friend Mistress Nora, she's the dominatrix I told you about. And her master, Mister S, he's this guy." She held out her arm to display the cross tattoo. "I'm close with them both. Anyway, the way she explained it was that for her, it was like being a surgeon."

"A surgeon?"

"A surgeon isn't always performing surgeries. But a really good surgeon is almost always on-call. So even if Doctor Surgeon is home with his kids or asleep or in the shower or on a date, if his pager goes off and he's needed in the operating room to save someone's life, then in a split second, he goes from

being Dad back to being Doctor Surgeon. Like that."
Simone snapped her fingers. "And that's how Nora
said it worked for them. She wasn't 'on' all the time,
but she was 'on-call' all the time. When Mister S
needed her or wanted her to serve him, she immediately dropped what she was doing and went and
served him."

"Yeah, but what if she couldn't? What if she was in
another state or working?"

"She said he respected her enough to not demand
that she serve him when she had something really
important going on. And even then, if she was, you
know, in another state when he needed her, she'd call
me, and I'd take care of business."

"Take care of business?"

"He's a sadist," she said. "If he needed to whip
somebody, well, he needed to whip somebody. And if
he needed it bad enough, he wasn't too picky about
who that somebody was. That's not true. He was really
picky. He just happened to pick me," she said
with pride.

Jason laughed. "So you were the substitute slave?"

"I was. And you better believe I had a lot of compe-
tition for that job."

"Good-looking guy, huh?"

"Not bad if you like incredibly handsome, six-foot-
four blond men."

"Not my type," he said. "Guess he was yours if you
got a tattoo for him."

"Keep up the good work, sir, and you'll earn some ink, too," she said.

"Good to have a goal." He pulled her closer to him.

"Of course...if you showed up at the club with your crop in your hand, there'd be a line around the block of subs, slaves, and masochists waiting their turn for you."

"And what's the address of this club of yours?" Jason asked.

She looked up at him, eyes narrowed and glaring.

"Oh, look at that—Spanky's got a jealous streak," he said. "I like that."

"I saw you first," she said, face scrunched up in determination.

"But you're my slave. I'm not your slave. Right?"

"Yes, master," she said, grinning.

"So I can play with anyone I want but you have to do everything I say?"

"No, master." She shook her head.

"No? Did you tell me no? You're going to get punished for that now."

He grabbed the dish towel off the counter. It was damp enough that when he twirled it and smacked her thigh with it, she let out a yelp that probably spooked the horses.

"Oh, shit," she said, laughing. "That stung like a bee."

"What did I say about swearing?"

He swatted her with the damp towel again. She

jumped a foot in the air, laughing and squealing at the same time.

"You keep doing that and I won't need to get a tattoo for you. I'll have a permanent scar," she said, trying to snatch the towel from his hand. She was laughing but he wasn't.

"Did I hit you too hard?" he asked, suddenly cold all over.

"What? No. I mean, it stung, but I'm okay."

"You said I was going to leave a scar on you."

"It's okay," she said. "I was kidding."

"Let me see it, Simone," he said, his voice so stern it almost scared him.

She looked surprised, almost scared, but she did as he'd ordered. She turned and lifted his shirt up to show him her upper right thigh.

Jason knelt down behind her and looked at the red mark he'd left on her leg. It was an angry red welt an inch long with a little bit of blood rushing to the surface.

"Jesus, I broke your skin," he said.

"So?"

"So?" he repeated. "Are you kidding me? You're bleeding."

She shrugged. "Happened before."

"Not with me."

"Yeah, but—"

"I have some antibiotic ointment and Band-Aids in the bathroom. I'll go get it."

He got up and left her in the kitchen. He heard her calling his name and ignored it. He nearly ran through his bedroom to get to the bathroom where he found his first aid kit. As he was heading back down he nearly ran into Simone coming up the steps.

"I got the stuff," he said. "Let's go in here and I'll clean you up."

She looked at him like he'd gone crazy but when he pointed at the door to the guest room, she went inside without a protest.

Simone lay on her stomach on the bed. Jason opened the first aid kit and set it up on the nightstand.

"I've got alcohol wipes," he said. "It'll sting a little."

"I can handle it," she said.

She didn't wince or flinch when he started cleaning the bloody welt. He did, though. The whole area around the welt was bright red and he could already tell she was going to have a bruise.

"I'm not sure a band aid will stay on that part of your leg very well," Jason said. "But we can try."

"Is it still bleeding?"

"Looks like it's stopped."

"Then I don't need a Band-Aid."

"You'll need some ice, though. I've got an ice pack around here—"

"Jason—"

"Or I can run to the drugstore for—"

"Jason."

Simone turned over and sat up. She met his eyes and said nothing.

Jason tossed the antibiotic ointment tube back onto the nightstand.

Simone smiled at him. "I've had worse," she said. "Way worse."

"I know," he said softly. "But I've...I've never done worse."

She reached for his hand, and he went down on his knees in front of her and rested his head in her lap.

"Sorry, baby," he said.

"It's fine, Jason. It really is."

Simone lightly scored his naked back and shoulders with her fingernails. He closed his eyes and tried to enjoy it. He hadn't had a girlfriend since before his career-ending injury put him in the hospital for a month. And that was nearly eighteen months ago. Long time since he'd had a good backscratching.

"Can I tell you something about women?" Simone asked.

"Tell me anything you want," he said.

"This might blow your mind a little, but I think you need to know the secret about us."

"What's the secret?"

"Here it is. It's a big one. The secret about women is...they're people."

Jason looked up at her. "You don't say."

"I'm not kidding," Simone said, not smiling. "We're people just like men are people."

"You know I know that, right?"

"I'm not sure you do," she said. "I think your dad might think women are like, I don't know, another species. A lot of men do. A lot of men think women are 'women' and men are people. I mean, don't get me wrong, there's nothing bad about a father teaching a son not to hit women. Better than the opposite. But I'm not some ideal concept of 'Woman,'" Simone said, putting "Woman" in finger quotes. "I'm a real, live flesh-and-blood woman. I'm Simone Levine. I'm from New Canaan, Connecticut. My dad's an insurance exec. My mom's a history professor. I have a sister five years older who owns a boutique organic pet food store. When I was eighteen, this hot young Wall Street punk I met at a coffee shop tried to shock me by taking me to a kink club on our first and only date. I shocked him by ignoring him the whole time to talk to the sexy French guy who owned the place. Two years later I was working at that club. Look, Jason," Simone said, smiling down at him. "I think I could go crazy about you pretty fast, but I'm not going to get involved with a guy who treats women like they'll break if you so much as breathe on them. If you want to respect women, respect the real woman in front of you, not some fake fantasy idea of what woman are supposed to be like. I'm a professional submissive and proud of it. Men— rich, important men—pay me two hundred dollars an hour to flog me, cane me, and whip me. I earn every penny and I love my job. I want you to treat me like your slave, but only if you can also treat me like an adult. You can call me 'baby' because it makes me wet. Don't call me 'baby' because you think I'm a child. I've gotten hurt worse than this stepping on a Lego. So there."

8

"So there?" Jason said.

"Tada?" Simone waved her hands in the air.

He smiled and shook his head.

"You're something, all right," he said. "What that something is I don't know, but I know I like it."

She took his face in her hands, bent and kissed him on the lips.

"I like you, too. A lot," she said. Then she added, "Sir."

Simone was relieved to see Jason had lost that deer-in-the-headlights expression he'd been wearing since he'd seen the blood on her thigh.

"I told you I don't have any idea what I'm doing," he said.

"It's your first day," she said. Had she ever met a man who was harder on himself than her kinky cowboy? "Could you stay on a bull the first time you rode one?"

"Got thrown before I was even out of the chute."

"See? Everything has a learning curve. I was a crappy submissive when I started. Took me a couple months to learn the ropes. Literally. Rope-play made me really claustrophobic at first. Now I love it. You just need practice."

Jason sat back on his knees. "When I was learning to ride bulls," he said, "only person I had to worry about getting hurt was me."

"If it makes you feel any better," she said, "I'd rather be with a dominant or a sadist or a master who worries way too much about hurting me than worries way too little. I've been with guys like that. I'll take you over them any night of the week." Simone meant every word of that. Jason's concern for her, misguided as it was, touched her heart.

"Including tonight?"

"Definitely tonight."

"It's a good thing I found you," he said. Simone's heart fluttered. "I need a pro to practice on before I inflict myself on some poor girl who's never done this before."

Simone felt a sudden pain in her stomach, like a knot tightening. Jason mentioning being with another girl had caused that knot. Pull it together, Simone scolded herself. After all, she was the one who told

Jason to treat this like practice so he'd be ready when he had a girlfriend again someday.

"Of course," she said. "Just practice. We all have to start somewhere."

"You sure about doing this with me?" he asked.

"Must be sure," she said. "I changed my flight for you, remember?"

"What am I gonna do with you for three nights?" he asked.

"The possibilities are endless," she said.

"Any suggestions? Am I allowed to ask?"

"You're the master here," she said. "You're allowed to do anything you want."

"Oh yeah." He grinned. "I keep forgetting that."

"Don't worry. I'll remind you."

"I think I've got a pretty good idea what to do with you right about now," he said.

"Your wish is my command."

"Lay on your back and open your legs," he said. Simone was more than happy to oblige.

He draped her legs over his shoulders and opened her pussy up for him with his fingers. If Simone thought Jason looked sexy while drying dishes wearing nothing but jeans and a smile, she didn't have the words to describe how good he looked while eating her pussy like his life depended on it. His brown eyes flicked upward to watch her watching him. He somehow managed to smile a dirty wicked smile even while rubbing his tongue over her swollen, tingling labia. He pressed two fingers into her and up against the tender spot on the front wall of her vagina and rubbed and rubbed and rubbed it while he licked and licked and licked her. The sounds coming out of Simone's throat might have woken the dead.

Simone could barely lie still as he swirled his tongue around her clitoris over and over again. He might be new at playing master but the man knew how to eat pussy, God bless him. As he fucked her with his fingers, she panted and moaned and begged for his cock.

"Not yet, Spanky," he said before going at her again with even greater intensity. The man was trying to kill her. No doubt about it. This was a murder attempt and that was fine by her. If she was going to die, let it be with Jason Waters' fingers on her G-spot and his tongue on her clit.

Her climax built up fast and there was no stopping it when it came. She cried out, her shoulders coming off the bed as he bore down on her mercilessly until she went limp, completely limp, on the bed and her legs slid lifelessly off his shoulders.

Jason stood up and leaned over her, examining her with a curious expression on his face.

"You all right there, Spanky?" he asked.

"You killed me dead. Put on my tombstone, 'Here lies Spanky Levine, done to death by her master's cruelty.'"

"Cruelty? I made you come so loud my ears are

ringing."

"You didn't put your cock in me," she said. "That's cruelty."

"It's my cock, not yours, and I'll put it in you on my say so, not yours."

Simone raised her head and met his eyes. "Ooh..." she said. "That was very sexy, sir."

"Come on," he said and dragged her by the arm to her feet. "You still have my come all over you. We need to wash that off."

"Shower time?" she asked.

"For you. You shower. I watch."

He pulled her down the hall to a door at the end. The bathroom, no doubt. But Simone dug her heels in at another door opposite the guest room.

"Is this your room?" she asked.

"Yeah."

"Can I see it?"

"It's messy," he said. "I have a bunch of junk in there."

"Why do I find that hard to believe?" she asked.

He turned around and stood at his bedroom door. He sighed.

"It's just...it's a bunch of stuff I don't quite know what do to with yet."

"I'm very good at organizing," she said. "Maybe I can help."

"You good at carpentry?"

"Not my strongest suit."

"Then you probably can't help. See?" He opened the door and flipped on the light switch. Simone did a double take, blinked and looked at Jason in shock.

"Holy crap," she said. Then added, "Am I allowed to say 'crap'?"

"You can say 'crap.'"

"Holy shit," she said. He pinched her ass in punishment. Simone walked into the room, jaw slightly open as she gazed in amazement at the massive collection of trophies, cups, ribbons, medals, and what appeared to be gold-plated and enormous belt buckles piled along the wall of his bedroom.

There had to be at least one ton of prizes just sitting on the floor.

"These all yours?" she asked. She'd seen fewer trophies in her high school's trophy case and that was for the entire school.

"They got my name on 'em."

Simone knelt on the floor in front of the collection.

"This is incredible, Jason. You must be so proud of yourself." She saw several trophies and cups that read "World Champion" among other equally impressive accolades. A decade's worth of achievement. And all just sitting on his bedroom floor.

"I had a good career," he said simply. "Glad it's over, and I'm still standing."

"So modest," she said, grinning. "Why do all these say PBR? Was Pabst Blue Ribbon beer a big sponsor?"

Jason laughed. "PBR. Professional Bull Riding. Although you're not the first to ask that."

"Are you planning on building a trophy case or something?" Simone asked as she sat back and carefully examined some of his prizes.

"Aimee told me to," he said, dropping down on the floor next to her. "But it's not my style. I don't want all this stuff in my living room."

"Got a spare room?"

"I don't want it in either of the guest rooms either. It's just too much. I was going to store it all up in the attic until Aimee chewed my ear off for even suggesting it."

"Maybe your old high school would take it? Or a museum? Are there cowboy museums? Rodeo museums?"

"My high school would love to have it," he said. "But Aimee'd still kill me if I chucked it all, even to them."

"Well, it's your stuff and your house. You get to decide what to do with it. Although I think you should wear this every day." She picked up a shiny diamond-encrusted belt buckle that was literally as big as her head.

"If I ever need a jockstrap and don't have one," Jason said, "I'll use this."

He took the buckle back from her and put it in the pile.

Simone finally wrenched her gaze from the

massive, and somewhat garish, collection of trophies and cups. As impressive as they were, she wouldn't want them on display in her living room, either.

She studied Jason's bedroom and found it to her liking. The floor was stained a nice light gray and the walls a darker gray. A large casement window looked out onto his pastures. And, she was pleased to see, one entire wall was covered in photographs—pictures of his family, his friends and his horses, all of them in rough wood frames of various sizes. The bed was king-sized with an old-fashioned iron headboard and foot-board, the kind with vertical bars kinky people favored since they made tying someone to the bed so very easy.

"You do the decorating in here?" she asked.

"Aimee might act like she owns the place when she visits, but not even she's allowed in my bedroom," he said.

"I love your photographs," Simone said. She stood up and looked at the wall of pictures. She picked out his parents easily. His mother—petite, gray-haired, pretty even in her farm clothes—smiled happily at the taller, broad-shouldered older man next to her. Jason's father didn't smile much. Like father, like son. In one photograph, Jason stood with a woman about his age with dark brown hair and a wide grin.

"Aimee?" Simone asked.

"That's us," he said. "That's my old house in the background there. Mom and Dad's house, I mean."

"Have they visited you yet?" Simone asked.

"Not yet but they're talking about it," Jason said. "Mom's still not thrilled I moved all the way out here."

"And your Dad?"

"He respects it. Told Mom to stop trying to tie me to her apron."

Simone turned to him and saw his eyes still on the photograph of his parents and their cattle ranch. She studied a different photograph of him and his sister. It looked like it was taken ten years ago. They were both holding trophies—his for bull riding, hers for barrel-racing.

"Your life looks so picture perfect," Simone said. "Like some kind of Montana fairy tale."

"Looks that way, I guess. Never felt that way."

"How did it feel?"

"Like I was trying to be perfect," he said. "Playing the part."

"You played it pretty well," Simone said, nodding meaningfully at his trophies and cups.

He gave her a tired smile. "I only got into bull riding because me and Uncle Vince got along so much better than me and Dad when I was in high school. But I guess that's normal. Most fathers and sons butt heads at that age. Just when you butt heads with a man like my father, only one of you walks away. The other crawls."

It sounded like Jason was trying to explain away his unhappiness, blame it on the nature of father/son relationships instead of admitting that his father had crossed a line and harmed his son.

"Why did you move out here? Really?" she asked. "I know Montana has horses. There's one right there." She pointed at a photograph of Jason's sister on a big black horse riding in the midst of a massive herd of cattle.

"Soon as I retired and recovered from this," Jason said, pointing at the scar on his stomach, "Mom and Aimee kind of took it upon themselves to find me a wife."

"A wife? Are you serious?"

"I want to get married one day," he said as if that were the most obvious thing in the world. "But I need to do things my own way. I couldn't go to dinner at Aimee's or go to church with Mom without either of them trying to set me up with some new girl."

"You know some of those women might have been kinky," Simone said. "Or open to trying it with you."

"Maybe so, but I know I'd never feel like I could do that there with them. Not with my family breathing down my neck and Aimee trying to be best friends with every girl I so much as had a beer with. When your family is close as mine is, too close sometimes, the only way to get any privacy is to move halfway across the country."

"I can see that," she said. "My family knows better than to ask me about my personal life anymore. I tell them if I find someone, they'll know when they get a rainbow-striped wedding invitation in the mail, and until that time to mind their own."

"Does that work?"

"Like a charm. Trust me, you drop a couple hints that you're kinky, your parents stop asking about your love life really fast."

"Mine would probably put me in a mental hospital."

"I would bust you out," she said. "Me and Rusty. We'd ride off into the sunset, all three of us. And we'll be as kinky as the day is long." She put her arm around his waist and rested her head on his shoulder.

"I don't know if Rusty'd be into that," Jason asked.

"Well, fine. He can be vanilla. We'll be kinky."

"I like that plan," Jason said. "That's a good plan. But I have a better one."

"What's that?"

Jason took her by the hips and steered her toward the door of the master bathroom.

"Oh yeah," she said. "Showering with an audience."

The bathroom was nice, as modern as the bedroom was old-fashioned. Jason turned on the water in the big glass shower stall and Simone stood there passively as he took his shirt off of her and dropped it onto the floor.

"In," he said.

"Yes, sir," she said, smiling. Naked, she stepped under the steaming water to wet her hair.

She didn't try to put on a good show for him. Fact

was, she really needed a shower and if he wanted to watch, he could watch. Fine by her. She found his soap and lathered it up in her hands and proceeded to rub it all over her chest, breasts, and stomach. She closed her eyes and put her face under the spray and wasn't the least bit surprised when she opened her eyes again to find Jason in the shower with her. Naked and happy to see her.

"I thought you were only watching, sir."

He pulled her to him. He was hard and she smiled as his erection pressed into her stomach. With a hand in her wet hair he tilted her head back, way back and kissed her neck, nibbled her earlobe, licked the water off her skin. He put his mouth to her ear.

"I'm in charge," he said. "I make the plans. I can change the plans."

This was a much better plan.

9

After their shower, it was close to bedtime, and Jason was just not sure what to do about that. Simone sat near the foot of the bed, naked but for his flannel shirt she'd put back on after the shower. She was toweling her wet hair and he was having trouble taking his eyes off her as she made herself at home in his room. She looked so damn cute, with her pink hair all wet and her bare legs sticking out from his shirt, that he could have stared at her all night.

"You need a hairdryer? Aimee left one in the guest bathroom," Jason said, feeling like a voyeur just standing there in the bathroom doorway watching her get ready for bed. It was so easy to be with her when they were naked and fooling around. Soon as it was over though, he started to question everything he said and did.

"My hair air-dries fast," she said. "But thank you, sir." She grinned at him.

"Aw...you gotta stop smiling at me like that and calling me sir," he said. "You're gonna give me ideas."

"Nothing wrong with ideas," she said. "And I'll call you 'sir' when you want me to and I won't when you don't. We don't have to be 'on' all the time."

He came out of the bathroom doorway. He had on his jeans and nothing else, which Simone had said was a very good look for him. Scars and all. He pulled the one chair in the room over in front of Simone, turned it around, and straddled it to face her.

"What am I gonna do with you?" he asked. "You make me feel too good."

"Well, this is what I think you should do with me," she said. "But you're in charge, so take it or leave it. I think you should relax and enjoy having me here as long as I'm here. I think you should feel free to ask me any questions you want to ask about kink or anything else on your mind. I think you should spank me and crop me and have sex with me whenever you feel like it. And I think you should let me sleep in here with you tonight."

"You think, Spanky? You don't think that's too soon?" he asked though he'd already decided that if she wanted to sleep with him, he'd let her.

"We only have a few days together so you might as well get all the master-practice in you can. And it'll be a lot easier for me to serve you," she said, reaching out to poke him right in the nose, "if I'm near you. Sir."

"I'm never gonna get tired of hearing you talk about 'serving' me." That was a fact. Every time she called him "sir" or "master" or said she wanted to "serve" him, a bolt of lightning hit him right in the solar plexus. He caressed her bare thigh with his hand for no other reason than he wanted to and he could.

"Keep being as sexy and fun and sweet as you are," Simone said, "and I'll never get tired of serving you."

"You really having fun with this?" he asked, if only to hear her say "yes" again.

"I am, Jason," she said softly as she looked into his eyes. "And I really mean it. This is...this is good, what you and I are doing. You feel that, right? That it's a good thing? Not a bad and dirty thing?"

"Well...a little dirty," he said, laughing. He'd ordered her to suck his cock and then he'd come on her breasts and fucked her after. If that wasn't dirty, what was?

"Only the good kind of dirty," she said. "Right?"

"I feel..." He took a hard slow breath. "I feel like if we keep doing this a few more days, I could get there. You know, feeling like it's good and not the sort of thing I ought to be ashamed of."

"But you're not there yet?" she asked.

He smiled at her, squeezed her knee. "Getting there," he said. "Trying."

"All I can ask," she said. She leaned in and kissed

him on the cheek. It was exactly the sort of kiss he needed right at that moment. A sweet kiss, not the least bit dirty. A sweet kiss from a sweet girl.

"Well, I'm exhausted. Someone wore me and my pussy out," she said. "So what are your orders, Mr. Waters? I'll sleep wherever you tell me to sleep."

"Well, better bunk with me," he said. "I've never had a pink-haired gal in my house. No telling what your sort gets up to in the night."

"We can be awfully wily," she said. "You should probably hold me really tight, in case I try to sneak out and get up to no good."

"If I hold you real tight tonight, we'll probably get down to no good."

"Then it's a win for both of us, sir."

Jason stripped out of his jeans and got into bed. Simone started to take off his flannel shirt but he told her to leave it on. He couldn't get over how sexy she looked in it. And if they were going to get a wink of sleep, she better keep those beautiful breasts of hers covered up for the time being.

Simone lay on her back and Jason lay close, resting his arm over her stomach like he was keeping her prisoner.

"You comfortable, Spanky?" he asked her.

"Very. You, sir?"

Comfortable? He had a beautiful girl in his bed wearing his shirt and calling him "sir" and eager to please him any want he wanted.

"Safe to say I'm about as comfortable as I've ever been in my life."

He kissed her one last time and fell fast asleep.

Around three am Jason woke up, his bladder's doing. He went to the bathroom without waking Simone up but once he was back in bed with her, he couldn't quite talk himself into closing his eyes and falling back to sleep. The moon was high and bright and he could see her on the pillow next to him. She looked so damn pretty curled up on her side, pink curls falling over her cheek, tangled in his sheets and breathing heavy. Jason still couldn't quite believe his luck. That stupid calendar thing was the last thing he'd wanted to do, yet it had brought this girl into his life, who seemed to know exactly what to say and do to make him feel like the man he'd always wanted to be. A strong man. The kind of man a woman wanted to please. The kind of man who knew how to keep a wild gal like this in hand. Just telling her to mind her manners, to say "thank you" and call him "sir," made him so hard his cock ached just thinking about it. In his old fantasies, the girls he'd done that sort of thing to—ordered them around, forced himself on them— submitted to him out of fear and respect. And while that was fine for a jack-off fantasy, this girl seemed to submit to him for another reason—because she loved doing it. For her own sake, and not just his. He could tell she respected him, was attracted to him, and all that was good but even better...she was having as much fun as he was doing all this crazy kinky stuff. And if he liked it and she liked it and they liked it together...then maybe it wasn't so crazy after all.

Before he even thought about what he was doing, Jason reached out and took her in his arms. He didn't mean to wake her up or startle her. He just needed her skin on his skin. Of course there was no way to drag a girl a foot across the bed at three in the morning without waking her up.

"Jason?" Simone said in a sleepy voice. "Is it morning?"

"Not yet, baby," he said softly, not wanting to wake her up any more than he already had. And yet, despite that noble intention, he kissed her on the mouth. She murmured a little sound of pleasure and opened her lips a little wider. He deepened the kiss, slipping his tongue inside her mouth and his hand under her— well, his—shirt. He stroked her side, her soft naked hips as he kissed her. And before he knew it, he had his fingers on the buttons of the shirt and they were coming open one by one...

"Sir?" she said, eyes still closed but grinning.

"I want you to serve me," he said as he opened the shirt and unveiled her breasts. She might still be half-asleep but he was rock hard and awake and alert as he'd ever been.

"Any way you want. Anything you want."

Those promises were the sexiest words he'd ever heard, and to hear them in her sleepy little voice just about did him in. He took her breast in his hand and squeezed, lifted it, and latched on to her nipple. He wasn't sure if he'd ever sucked a girl so hard before. He'd been trained to be gentle but it didn't seem like Simone had much use for gentle. Her head fell back as he pinched her other nipple, pulled it and rubbed it over and over with his thumb. He moved on top of her to have better access. He licked her nipples and massaged her breasts until she was panting like a horse that had just won the Kentucky Derby. Jason's own heart was pounding a million miles a minute and his cock throbbed. He had to get into her or he'd die. He cupped her between her legs and stroked the seam of her pussy. He felt heat, wet heat, so he parted the folds and plunged his fingers inside her. Simone shuddered as he penetrated her; she lifted her hips for him.

"You better open your legs for me," he said.

"I'll open anything you want me to," she said.

"Who does this pussy belong to?" Jason rasped into her ear as he pushed his fingers deeper into her. Her inner muscles clenched around his fingers.

"You, sir."

"You better fucking believe it," he said, words wild and dirty enough even Simone gasped.

He spread his fingers wide inside her pussy, opening her up for him.

"Oh, you like that," he said as she flinched when he touched a tight knot of muscle in her.

"Feels so good..." she said.

"I'm going to spend the next three days getting to know everything there is to know about your pussy. And you're gonna know my cock better than you know your own name before it's over."

Jason kissed her before she could say a word and he only broke the kiss to lean up and grab a condom off the nightstand. He was so aroused he was almost shaking and he had to take a deep breath to get the condom rolled on. Once it was on, he didn't waste another second. Using his knees, he forced Simone's thighs wide. He slipped his arm around her back, lifted her to his chest, and rammed his cock into the wet hole of his dreams.

Obedient as she was, Jason didn't even have to tie Simone's wrists to the headboard. She grabbed the bottom bar with both hands and held on while he fucked her. He was on his elbows over her, leaving just enough space between their bodies that he could ram his cock into her good and hard. He wanted her to feel every inch of it. He wanted it to rub her swollen clit until she came apart under him. And he told her all that while Simone lay there under him, taking it and taking it. On her back, her breasts bare and swollen from sucking, her hands hanging onto the headboard, her head back and her eyes closed, she was the very picture of sexual surrender. But she was no passive slave, putting up with her master's demands out of fear and obedience. No, she had her heels dug into the bed and she was lifting her hips up every time he pounded down into her.

Never once in his entire twenty-nine years had he woken up a girl in his bed for the sole purpose of fucking her. He'd fantasized about it, fantasized about having a beautiful, obedient sex slave he could use at will—night or day—but this was different. This wasn't some nameless, faceless fantasy girl. This was a real woman who was letting him use her pussy at three in the god-damned morning. He rubbed her breasts and her belly, savoring the softness of her skin, her curves, her heat, and most of all, her total submission to him and his cock.

"Ride me," he ordered as he rolled onto his back, bringing her with him. She put her hands on his chest to steady herself as she rose up, his cock still deep inside her. Simone rocked her hips against him and her head fell back in pleasure as he took her breasts in his hands and held them. He fucked her from under her, lifting her on his cock as he rubbed her nipples until they were hard as diamonds. Her head dropped to her chest and she groaned. He saw her eyes barely open through the wild curls of her hair and he had to make her come. He had to or he'd never forgive himself. He slid one hand down her body, down her belly, and held her by the hip.

"Come for me, baby," he said as he rubbed her clit with his thumb. "That's an order now."

He was either real damn good at rubbing her clit or she was real damn good at taking orders—or both— because she went stiff on top of him, her hips frozen in mid-pump. He felt her tight wet vagina clench all around his cock, clench and contract, and he let out a stream of profanity to make the angels weep when he felt her orgasm. He almost lost control of himself and came before he wanted to. As soon as she went limp on top of him, he brought her back down to the bed and onto her stomach. He took her hips in his hands, lifted them, and entered her from behind. She'd already come. She was wiped out. She was one and done and he didn't care one bit. He would use her pussy for the next two hours if he wanted to, if that's what it took. Because he could. Because she'd told him that hole belonged to him and he believed her. His cock certainly believed her as he thrust into her hard and fast over and over again until he was on the edge of coming and even a stiff breeze would push him over.

He didn't get a stiff breeze but he did get Simone moaning under him, moaning a low, slow "Oh, God, sir..." And that was all the help he needed. He pumped a few more times into her and then it was on. Semen shot out of him hard as it ever had, even harder maybe, and it felt like he was going to come until he was dead. Muscles he'd forgotten he had clenched, and nerves he'd never met before fired in his stomach and hips and thighs. He fucked her and came and fucked her and came some more and when he was done coming, he collapsed onto her body, his penis still inside her, quickly going soft. He caught his breath and pulled himself up and off of her. He went to the bathroom, took care of the condom, and crawled back into bed. He spooned up behind Simone and put his arm over her, holding her close.

"You enjoy that, Spanky?" he asked, but got no answer.

She was already sound asleep.

Jason laughed softly. He had knocked her right out. And he was about ten seconds from sleep himself. In those last ten seconds before he fell asleep, he had a thought. And that thought was this: if he wasn't careful, he was going to get real used to this real damn fast.

And that was going to be a real problem once Simone left.

So maybe he ought not to let her leave.

And after that bright idea, Jason fell asleep, too.

10

Jason woke up early to check on the horses before Franco arrived at nine. Usually he got out of bed immediately upon waking. This morning he had a reason to linger. Simone lay on her side facing the window. Her naked back was way too tempting. All he wanted to do was press himself against her until she woke up, and they could have sex again.

The horses might not appreciate that, however.

Jason threw on clothes, walked the barns, let the crisp April morning air wake him up better than coffee ever could. Maybe it was last night's rain. Maybe the sky was more blue than usual that day. Maybe he had on rose-colored glasses because he had a pretty pink-haired girl in his bed who kept calling him "sir." But whatever the reason, Jason decided today was the nicest day he'd spent yet in Kentucky.

God damn, he loved it here. He loved his hundred-year-old farmhouse hidden among the oak trees, loved every inch of his sixty-acre spread. Good thing Franco wasn't there or Jason might have hugged the man and that might have made their working relationship a little awkward.

Leaning on the wooden fence, he watched the horses for a few minutes. Rusty and Barley, the trail horse he'd been training, were making friends over a patch of clover. A few heavy limbs on the eighty-foot oak tree in the center of the pasture had come down during the rain yesterday. Jason made a note to tell Franco to call the tree guys to come trim the branches.

Otherwise everything looked good. Nothing more for him to do except go back to the house and see about getting Simone out of bed. Or maybe leaving her in there all day. Of course if she was in bed all day, he couldn't leave her there alone. She'd need company. Otherwise she'd get bored. God only knew what sort of trouble a pink-haired New York gal would get into if he left her alone for too long.

He kicked off his wet boots in the mudroom before heading upstairs to see what his girl was up to.

His girl?

Well, for a couple days she was his girl. All his and no one else's. He still couldn't quite believe he'd found her and in the craziest of places—the library. He ought to check out books more often if this was the sort of thing that went on in libraries.

Back in his bedroom he found Simone still sleeping, tangled up in his red flannel sheets and covered up to the neck in his plaid quilt.

"You awake, Spanky?" he asked, tugging the quilt down to see her face.

"If you tell me to wake up, I'll wake up," she said with her eyes still closed tight. "But if you don't, I'm sleeping." She gently and slowly pulled the quilt back over her face. Jason laughed and tugged it down again.

"Gotta wake up," he said. "That's an order."

Over the top edge of the blanket she opened her eyes.

"See? There's a good girl," he said.

"You're up early, sir."

"It's eight. Not that early."

"It's early for me. Especially since my wicked master woke me up at three in the morning to f—"

He glared at her.

"To have sexual relations with me," she said.

"You weren't complaining last night."

"I'm not complaining this morning, either." She grinned up at him. "It's my job, after all."

"It is," he said. He pushed the covers down to her waist for no other reason than she had gorgeous breasts and he wanted to look at them. "And you're very good at your job."

He bent his head and kissed her nipples. Simone murmured soft sounds of pleasure as she put her hand around his neck and caressed his hair.

He moved up her chest and neck to her lips and gave her one long lingering kiss.

"Good morning," he said.

"Good morning, sir."

"Now get your ass out of bed and dressed. Be in the kitchen in five minutes or else."

"Or else what?" she asked.

"You challenging me?" he asked, staring down at her.

"No, but I don't know if I can get cute in five minutes so I'm just wondering what the consequences are if I'm late."

Jason looked up at the ceiling.

"Lord, give me the patience to put up with pink-haired girls and their sass."

Then he ripped the covers off her, dragged her over his legs and spanked her hard and fast about half a dozen times, Simone laughing and squealing the entire time. When finished he playfully threw her off his lap and back onto the bed. He stood up and pointed down at her.

"Five minutes," he said. "Starting now."

As he left the bedroom he saw her jump out of the bed.

"I have no clothes," she said.

"Not my problem," he called back.

He smiled all the way down the stairs. There were worse things in life than driving a sexy girl up the wall before breakfast.

Jason had just poured the coffee when Simone appeared in the kitchen wearing one of his flannel shirts from his closet, a pair of his socks, and nothing else.

"You stole my panties," she said when he looked her up and down over the top of his coffee mug.

"I'm keeping 'em, too," he said. "What are you wearing under there?"

"Boxers," she said and lifted her shirt to show him. "Yours, sir."

"Cute. Real cute. I guess we need to get your luggage out of the car."

"I don't know. I like wearing your clothes," she said. "Nice and cozy."

"We got another option," he said.

"What's that?"

"I could keep you naked all week."

He was pleased to see that idea didn't horrify her.

"If that's what you want," she said with a smile. "Sir."

"You'd get cold."

"Not if you kept me warm."

"You--" he pointed at her with his mug--"are killing me."

She raised her hands in feigned innocence. "Oops? Sorry?"

"You're about as sorry as I am. You get breakfast started. I assume you know how to cook bacon and eggs?"

"I can handle that."

"And I'll get your things out of your car," he said. "Can't have you running around the farm naked. I got good Christian neighbors."

Simone was already digging through his fridge when he went to put his boots on to fetch her things from her car. Her car keys were on the kitchen table. As he walked to her car, he realized that at any point yesterday evening, last night, or this morning, she could have put her clothes on, her shoes—also still in the kitchen—and grabbed her keys and left.

But she hadn't left. He'd spanked her and cropped her, woken her up in the dead of night for the sole purpose of fucking her, and now he'd ordered her to cook them breakfast while he brought her things in. He'd even struck her so hard—accidentally—that she'd bled a little bit. And not once had she even hinted that she was thinking about running for it.

She was here. She was his—for the time being.

And she was sticking around.

He'd thought for sure that if he ever told a girl he liked what he was into, what he fantasized about, what he knew he needed if he was ever going to fall in love and stay in love, that girl would run for the hills like a pack of wild dogs was nipping at her heels. The girls in his fantasies were always crying, begging, pleading for mercy when he turned them over his knee or spanked them or forced them to perform sex acts on him and for him. He never knew there were women who'd sign up for that and do it with a smile.

But Simone had, and she was still there, in his kitchen, cooking breakfast and smiling because he'd come back with her things, and she was happy to see him.

"Orange juice?" she asked.

"Just coffee."

She poured the coffee and put the plates on the table.

"I could get used to this," he said as he sat her down at the table and took his seat opposite her.

"Someone to cook breakfast?" she asked. "I'm not that good of a cook."

"No, I mean, I could get used to feeling this good every morning. Instead of...I don't know, feeling alone all the time."

Simone gave him a soft-eyed smile. She really was awfully sweet.

"Mistress Nora told me there's different kinds of loneliness," she said. "There's the lonely where you're lonely for someone else. But there's also a kind of loneliness where you're lonely for your real self. You think you're missing someone in your life and it turns out it's you. Maybe you felt alone so much because you had to hide the real Jason from yourself for so long."

"Maybe so," he said. "It's kind of nice getting to be me."

"He's not such a bad guy," Simone said between bites of eggs over easy.

"I thought he was."

Simone shrugged. "I won't lie to you," she said. "Lots of women wouldn't like this. Being spanked by a guy as strong as you hurts. Blow jobs on command are not something a lot of women are 100% into. And being woken up at three in the morning so your guy can f...have sex with you would not fly in a lot of relationships. But, lucky for you, it flies with me."

"It flies, does it?"

"Like a 747."

"Why do you like it so much?" he asked.

"You really want to know?"

"I asked."

"Well, truth is, the reason I like it so much is...I'm awesome."

He laughed. "That so?"

"You think it's awesome, right? At least certain parts of you seem to think so?"

"And my opinion counts that much?"

"We're the only two people who exist in our little private world, remember? If I think I'm awesome and you think I'm awesome, who's to argue?"

"That's a damn good point," he said and went to work devouring his breakfast, which was better than he expected from a New Yorker.

"Can I tell you something else, sir?" Simone asked a minute or so later.

"I suppose you can."

"I think you're awesome, too."

She said it teasingly like the adorable tease she was, but it hit Jason hard right in the gut.

"Do you know how many women have said stuff like that to me?" he asked her.

Her eyes flashed wide. "A lot?"

He nodded. "You win big trophies and you win big money and you get a couple commercials for trucks, and girls who knew you six days in the fifth grade show up at your events and shove their phone numbers in your pocket while they're whispering in your ear how much they want to fuck you. I had girls offer me their prettier sisters if I'd take them first. I had a mom offer me herself and her daughter. Why is that when they say stuff like that to me, I think they're blowing smoke in my eyes and with you...with you I think I almost believe it?"

"Just like we talked about last night," Simone said. "People will say they respect 'women' and what they actually respect is some fantasy ideal of women that has almost nothing in common with the real women all around them. Those women who hit on you were like that. You were a fantasy to them, this famous rugged champion who never had a scared or insecure moment in his life. They were talking to the fantasy cowboy they saw. I was talking to Jason Waters sitting at this table with me. That's why you should believe me. And what you should believe is there's nothing wrong with what you are and a whole lot right with it. You might not be the sort of man for every woman out there but you are definitely a good man who is very sexy and a lot of fun to be with. And even more fun to serve, be it breakfast or blow jobs."

She ended her little speech with a toss of her hair and a too-innocent-to-be-believed smile.

Jason laughed. "Breakfast or blow jobs?"

"Exactly."

"What about breakfast *and* blow jobs?" he asked.

"What about it, sir? Sounds like a good morning to me."

Jason put his fork down and sat back in his chair. "Come here," he said. He pointed at the floor.

Simone stood up and gracefully knelt at his feet.

Jason unbuttoned his jeans.

She licked her lips and wrapped her mouth around his cock and sucked it until it was rock hard.

He could get used to mornings like this.

11

Simone's handsome master was oh-so-kind enough to allow her to finish getting cleaned up and dressed while he did the breakfast dishes. She was happy to see the little smile on his face as she left him in the kitchen at the sink. She dug through her bag and found her black leggings, a mostly clean red V-neck t-shirt and her favorite gray hoodie. She put on her makeup, tamed her hair, and made Jason's bed. While tucking in the corners, she eyed his pile of trophies. Maybe while she was here, she could help Jason figure out a better place for them than stacked on the floor.

Before heading out the door she checked her phone for messages. Nothing important, thank goodness. She was having the time of her life here and she prayed the real world would mind its own business for a few days. Just to be on the safe side, Simone sent her friend Nora a text giving her all the details of where she was and who she was with. She trusted Jason and doubted he'd hurt a fly, but she'd been trained to make sure someone always knew where she was, especially if kink was involved. Nora must have been awake already because she typed a reply immediately.

"**What the hell is it about Kentucky?**" Nora replied with a few shocked face emojis plus a horse or two. "**Got to be something in the water there. I had killer wall sex in Kentucky once. You?**"

"**Bed and floor only. Walls are next.**"

"**Nice. You like this guy?**" Nora wrote back.

"**Amazing spanker,**" Simone wrote. Then a more serious message followed. "**I think I could fall for him.**" Those were the scariest seven words she'd ever typed into a tiny message box on an iPhone.

"**Don't do it!**" Nora replied. "**Or do it. Just googled him. He's pretty. Fall for him and make sure he falls for you, too.**"

"**That's not helping,**" Simone replied. "**I'm trying not to fall in love with him.**"

"**If he's nice, sexy, and knows how to spank, what's stopping you?**"

Fair question.

Jason had ordered her to come out to the barn when she was finished getting ready. He'd cautioned her to wear shoes that would be easy to clean off. Maybe he was planning on making her clean out horse shit from the stalls. She decided against her white canvas sneakers and put on her leather boots instead. They weren't quite cowboy boots but they looked pretty darn good with leggings.

Simone pushed open the large barn door and found Jason standing outside a stall with a horse's head resting on his shoulder. Jason was brushing the horse's mane while he spoke in a low, soothing voice to the seemingly blissed-out animal.

"Who's your friend?" Simone asked as she came up to the stall.

"This is Cupcake," Jason said. "Cupcake, this is Simone."

"Can I pet her?" Simone asked.

"Put your hand out, palm down, and let her sniff it first."

Simone did as ordered. She grinned as Cupcake's hot horsy breath tickled the back of her hand. "Now you can pet her. Just stand to the side of her head, not in front, so she can see you better."

"Hi, Cupcake," Simone said as she reached over the stall door to gently stroke the horse along the side of her head and long neck.

"Cupcake here is a Welsh pony," Jason said. "Thirteen hands, which is pretty big for a Welshie."

"Pretty coat," Simone said. "A blonde."

"Buckskin," Jason said. "Cupcake belongs to a little girl named Katie who is getting her in one week for her eleventh birthday."

"Lucky Katie," Simone said.

"Katie's recovering from brain surgery after a car accident," Jason said, "and she's had a hard time learning how to talk again. But for some reason, she'll talk to horses. She lights up around them so her parents want her to have her own."

"Ah, so Cupcake's a therapy horse?"

"Right," Jason said. "And that's where you come in. Cupcake here's never been ridden by anyone of the female persuasion. We need to get her used to being around girls since she's going to have a girl of her own in a week. You want to take Cupcake for a spin? It would be doing me and Katie a favor."

"Count me in," Simone said.

"You ever ridden a horse before?"

"Nope."

"Perfect," Jason said. "Neither has Katie. You stand here by her head and talk to her and pet her while I saddle her up. Cupcake's gonna have to get used to a lot of female attention."

Jason led her into the stall and Simone did as instructed. Easiest orders she ever followed. Pet a pony and talk to it? Sign her up for that.

"Hi, Cupcake," Simone said as she ran her hand up and down the horse's long jawline. "You're cute. I hope Master Jason's been good to you. Does he give you treats? He gives me lots of treats."

"What are you telling that pony about me?" Jason asked as he put a blanket across Cupcake's back.

"We're having some girl talk," Simone said. "So it's none of your business, Mister."

Cupcake blew through her lips, making a "pppbbbt" sound.

"See?" Simone said. "Even Cupcake says to mind your own."

"I'm minding my own," Jason said, throwing the saddle on the pony's back.

"I've never ridden a pony before," Simone said. "Although I've done a little pony-play. Does that count? Probably not. I've worn a saddle but never been in a saddle. First time for everything."

Simone looked over and saw Jason staring at her with one eyebrow about an inch higher than the other.

"You want me to explain pony-play to you?" she asked him.

"Let me think about that and get back to you," he said. "You ready to ride?"

"Ready, sir. You ready, Cupcake? I never ride anyone without their consent first."

Cupcake batted her palm playfully.

"I think that's a yes," Simone said.

"That's a yes," Jason said. "Now I'm going to take her out to the paddock by the lead rope. I want you walking by my side, not behind her. Never get behind her. Then you'll get in the saddle. We'll do a few laps with me leading. You don't do anything but keep your hands on the saddle horn. I'm gonna be there the entire time. You want to stop and get off at any point just say the word—"

"Jellybeans," Simone said.

"That'll do. If for some reason, you feel yourself starting to fall, just fall. Land on your ass and roll away from Cupcake. Happens to everybody at least once riding. Don't fight the fall, and you'll get nothing more than a bruise or two if that."

"Then what?"

"Then you get back on the horse right away, or you'll be scared of horses the rest of your life."

"Got it."

Simone walked next to Jason as he led Cupcake out of her stall and into a round, fenced-in field which he called the paddock. The three of them simply walked one turn around the paddock together while Simone kept up the chatter with Jason and Cupcake. That was one of Jason's orders, too. Horses needed to get used to noise, to voices, to being startled so they could remain calm under stressful circumstances. Even more important for a pony like Cupcake who would soon belong to a little girl who'd never ridden before.

"Has Katie met Cupcake yet?"

"Oh yeah," Jason said. "Her parents asked me to find a couple candidates to be Katie's pony. They brought her out here to meet them and Cupcake was the horse Katie latched onto. I think it's going to be a good match."

"It's nice her parents can afford a horse and lessons and stuff. That's gotta add up."

Jason shrugged. "They're not rich but they have the barn and enough acreage to support a horse. That's all we ask."

"Who's we?"

"Nobody."

Simone eyed Jason suspiciously.

"Who is we, Master Jason?" she asked again. She knew calling him "Master" would do the trick.

"Oh, just a little thing me and a couple local families got going."

"Like a charity thing?" Simone asked. Jason shrugged. "Did you buy Cupcake for Katie?"

"Ponies don't cost much."

Simone laughed. "You totally bought a pony for a little girl. That's the sweetest thing ever."

"Don't have any kids yet," Jason said. "Gotta spoil somebody. You ready to get in the saddle?"

"Ready as I'll ever be."

"Left side," Jason said. "Left side on. Left side off. Every time. No exceptions. Left hand holds a tuft of mane. Left foot in the stirrup, right leg pushes up and swings over."

"Left foot in the stirrup," Simone repeated. "Right leg pushes up and swings."

"Fast and smooth," Jason said. "Don't think about it. Just do it."

Simone didn't think about it. She just did it. She

pushed off with her right foot and swung her leg over Cupcake's back. Before she realized she'd done it, she sat in the saddle.

"Wow, it's high up here," she said. She immediately felt wobbly.

"Yeah, and this is a little ole pony," Jason said. "You'd get the bends if you tried this on Rusty."

"Am I doing everything right?" Simone asked.

"So far. Put both your hands right there on the saddle horn," Jason said. Simone obeyed. "Now sit up straight as an arrow. Imagine you got an iron bar down the back of your shirt. Head against the bar. Shoulders against the bar. Tailbone against the bar."

"Wish I had my corset on," Simone said. "That would help with my posture."

"You got a corset?" Jason asked.

"Never leave home without it," she said. "Remember when I told you I did a little fetish modeling?"

"Yeah..." He sounded intrigued.

"Well, you put me in a corset and I turn into an hourglass so I make a pretty good corset model. I can show you the pictures. I take most of them myself."

"Corsets are a fetish?"

"For some people. Lots of dominant men like to truss up their ladies in corsets. It's very sexy to be corseted."

"And you said you have one with you?"

"Of course I do."

Jason smiled up at her. She loved that smile.

"Now I know what I'm doing with you tonight," he said, a threat and a promise. Simone got very warm inside at the thought of Jason yanking her laces tight. "Now I want you to sit there and look pretty while I lead Cupcake around."

Simone sat up even straighter and smiled.

"Am I doing it right?" she asked.

"What?"

"The 'sit there and look pretty' part?"

"World-class looking-pretty," he said before turning and clucking his tongue at Cupcake. Just like that the horse started walking at Jason's side. Simone stiffened in surprise as she swayed in the saddle. No wonder Jason had warned her about the possibility of falling off. Even on a pony in a paddock, this was a lot of rocking and swaying and Simone felt like her head was in the clouds.

"You all right back there, Spanky?" Jason said.

"I'm not going to faint, I promise. I didn't know horses were this, um...tall."

"You'll get used to it," he said.

"I think I am," she said. "Or I'm getting used to staring at your backside while you walk my horse around."

Jason wiggled his hips, and Simone burst out laughing. Luckily Cupcake was a well-trained pony and didn't bolt at the sound. Simone, however, nearly slid off the saddle and had to right herself quickly.

"You okay?" Jason asked.

"Your ass is dangerous," Simone said. "I better keep my eyes off it and on the road."

"Your ass is gonna get it later for swearing in front of a little girl's pony." Jason looked over her shoulder and winked at her. Simone nearly fell off her damn horse again at that naughty wink.

"So you get to threaten me with corseting and spanking in front of Cupcake, but I don't get to say 'ass'?"

"That's right."

"How is that fair?"

"It's not. But I'm your master and you're gonna follow my orders, fair or not. You got that?"

"I got it, sir," she said.

"Good."

As Jason led Cupcake around a barrel, Simone saw the smile on his lips.

She almost asked him to give an order right then and there.

She wanted him to order her not to fall in love with him.

A simple order to give.

Maybe an impossible one to follow.

12

They spent a good hour in the paddock, which was probably the limit of what Simone's backside could handle her first time in a saddle. He sure didn't want to wear her out. He had plans for that ass of hers later, saddle-sore or not.

He brought Cupcake to a halt and held her steady while Simone dismounted. Soon as her feet hit the ground, she wobbled unsteadily. Jason reached for her and held her against him while she found her footing.

"You all right?" he asked her, happier than he ought to be to have her back in his arms.

"Just have to get my sea legs," she said.

"You're on solid ground, Spanky."

"Then why is it moving?"

"That's your inner ear," he said and kissed her

quick on the lips. "You hold onto the fence and rest. I'll put Cupcake back in her stall."

Simone leaned back against the fence while Jason took care of Cupcake, getting her saddle off and settled in for the day. The pony had done better than he'd hoped. Not once had she startled, not even when Simone had burst out laughing when he shook his ass at her. When Cupcake was contentedly eating her oats, Jason went back out to the paddock where he found Simone texting someone.

"Something going on?" he asked.

"Oh, no, just telling my friend Nora I've ridden my first horse." Simone slipped her phone into her hoodie pocket.

"She, ah...she know you're here with me?" Jason asked.

"I told her."

"Did you tell her my name?"

"Well...yes," Simone said, a nervous smile flitting across her face. "I mean, it's a rule. When you do kink with a new person, you're supposed to tell a friend where you are and who you're with and when you're coming back. It's a safety thing. That's all."

"She won't tell anyone, will she? About me?"

"Oh, no." Simone shook her head quickly. "No, she's a pro, too. That's why we use each other as our safety calls when we travel for work. We're both trained to keep our mouths shut about clients and stuff. She won't tell a soul."

"That's good," he said.

"Are you embarrassed about being with me?" Simone asked.

Jason realized immediately he'd insulted the girl and entirely without meaning to, dammit.

"Spanky, I'd walk down Main Street America with you on my arm if I could. But if you saw the fan mail I get from kids, little kids, you'd know why I was worried about, you know, rumors getting out about me. When you got kids who look up to you, you have to keep your private life real private."

"I promise I won't start any rumors. I'm a professional, remember?" She didn't sound or look angry, only hurt that he'd think she was the sort to kiss and tell.

"Right. Of course. Never meant to imply otherwise." Jason kissed her again to clear the air between them. "I know you're a pro. I just didn't really think of myself as a client."

"Client or not, I think it's safe to say we're friends now, right?" she said. "I usually don't do kink or have sex with enemies. I won't betray your trust."

"I know you won't."

As soon as he said it, he realized he believed it. He wasn't just being nice. He did trust her. He must, right? He'd told her the one secret he'd never told anyone, the secret that scared even him.

"Come on," he said. "You need to go give Cupcake a treat. She earned it."

"What kind of treat?" Simone asked as they walked back into the barn.

"Cookies," he said. He grabbed a bucket off a shelf and passed it to Simone. She opened the lid and her nose immediately wrinkled.

"These are not Oreos," she said.

"They're horse cookies," Jason said. "Oats, rolled barley, dried apples, and molasses."

"Oh, that's not so bad." Simone sniffed the cookie. "Or maybe not."

"They're not shortbread," Jason said, "but Cupcake likes them. Don't you, girl?"

Cupcake already had her head out of the stall door and batted Simone's hand in eagerness. Jason knew how the little pony felt. He'd had a hard time not grinning like a fool all morning while he led Simone around the paddock. She'd been like a kid, so excited to get to ride her first horse. It was good for him to feel in charge like that, to teach her something for a change. And she was a good student, listened to every word he said and did as he asked. If she stuck around he'd turn her into a horsewoman in no time. She already had the most important part down—she wasn't afraid of horses. In fact, it seemed like his pink-haired lady wasn't afraid of much of anything.

"Put the cookie on your palm," Jason said. "Hold your hand out and watch your fingers. She can nip 'em by accident and then she'd feel bad for days if she bit your hand off."

"And I might need that hand later," Simone said.

"You just might," he said.

Simone did as he told her to and Cupcake lapped the cookie off her palm in one swish of her tongue.

"Agh!" she said and giggled. Her nose wrinkled and it was too damn cute for words. "That felt so weird."

"Never been licked by a horse before?" Jason asked.

"I've been licked by a man called Horse before, but that was an entirely different situation."

"Do I want to know why he was called Horse?" Jason asked.

"Your first guess is probably the right one."

Jason was the one bursting into laughter that time. Cupcake took it well.

While Simone petted and cooed over Cupcake, Jason stood by and watched. He could get used to this, having Simone out here in the barn with him, fussing over the horses, helping him out, keeping him company. But he highly doubted that was something Simone would want for herself. People who lived in New York City did so for a reason and you couldn't ask for a place more opposite her town than his. Nice fantasy, her staying here with him, but he knew better than to bet money on that. And it was probably just his cock doing the talking, anyway. For the first time in his life he was having the kind of sex he'd dreamed about. They barely knew each other, after all. Just met the day before. He knew people fell in love fast, at first sight even, but he'd never been that guy before. Then again, he'd never met a girl like Simone before.

"Well," he said with a sigh, "I gotta get to working. You won't be bored today while I'm out here?"

"No," she said between little kisses on Cupcake's forehead. "I have my laptop with me. I can get work done. I have a whole wedding album to organize. That'll take me two days at least."

"If you need me, you find me," he said.

"I'll find you. Sir."

She gave him one last smile before turning and walking out of the barn. He watched her go and enjoyed the view. Only view any better was her walking toward him. He stared long enough Cupcake bumped him in the shoulder with her head.

"Mind your own," Jason told the pony. "I can stare if I want to. She's mine."

Cupcake snorted at that.

"Sort of," he amended. "For now anyway. You think I oughta keep her?"

Cupcake didn't respond to that question at all except to blink her heavily lashed eyes a few times. Jason took that as a "maybe."

Franco arrived at ten and together the two of them put the horses through their paces. It made for hard work and a long day even with the two of them, but the hours flew by. When Franco made a passing reference to what a good mood Jason was in, Jason almost told him to "mind his own" before confessing that yes, he was in high spirits. Franco asked him why and Jason stole Simone's line from her.

"Your first guess is probably the right one."

Franco left shortly after six, and Jason finished up with the horses not long after. He was just getting Rusty his oats when he felt his phone vibrate in his back pocket. He pulled it out and answered, too preoccupied to even check who was calling him.

"Waters," Jason said.

"You asshole," were the first words he heard.

"Luke Bradley," Jason said. "To what do I owe the pleasure?"

"Did I mention you were an asshole?" Luke said.

"I think we covered that territory."

"You're not gonna ask why I'm calling you to tell you you're an asshole?" Luke asked.

"I'm sure you have your reasons," Jason said. He had a hidebound policy of not giving people who craved attention the attention they wanted. Drove them crazy.

"Naked calendar. Photo shoot. Yesterday," Luke said. "You were supposed to call and tell me how it went? Remember? You getting in the raw in front of that sexy-as-hell photographer from New York?"

"Hey, how do you know she's sexy as hell? You never met her," Jason said.

"Seen her pictures, man. Why do you think I agreed to be in the stupid calendar in the first place.

She's got a website. I've been on it. A lot. I'm on it right now. Oh my God..."

"Yeah, I'm gonna need you to stop doing that."

"Why?"

"Cuz I said so," Jason said. "And aren't you supposed to be in traction?"

"My dick's in traction after looking at her in her tight corsets."

"Dude, stop it, I swear to God."

"Whoa," Luke said, all joking over. "What the hell is going on, man? I just called to find out if she was as pretty in person as she is in her pictures."

"Yes, she's very pretty, and she's sweet, too. Don't talk about her like that to me. All right?"

A long pause followed.

"You fucked her," Luke said.

"I'm hanging up."

"You dirty dog, you did. God damn, I am killing myself as soon as we get off the phone. I gave that girl to you on a silver fucking platter."

"That's not how this works. What Simone and I did or did not do is none of your goddamned business, and if you keep talking about her like that, you're gonna be in traction for the rest of your life."

"I better get to be best man in the wedding, son."

"I'm going to a pallbearer in your funeral if you don't shut the hell up, *son*."

Luke laughed. "I'm only giving you a hard time, man. You make it too easy."

"Yeah, I know," Jason said. "I really like her."

"Don't blame ya. Just don't bring her home to your parents unless you want them to stroke out on the front porch. Mama Waters would hit the ceiling so hard the house would have a new skylight."

"She's just a pretty girl with pink hair. She doesn't have a swastika tattooed on her forehead."

"She's a pretty girl with pink hair who has a whole lot of crazy hot self-portraits on the internet, Jase. Which I will never ever look at again, I swear, cowboy's honor."

"Better not."

"But I remember..."

Jason hung up before he could say something he'd regret.

Fucking Luke Bradley. And Jason had been having one of the better days of his life before that bullshit phone call. Did the boy not have anything better to do than get online and perv over pictures of women he didn't know? Well, considering he was in traction in the hospital, probably not.

He returned to the house, kicked his boots off in the mudroom, and went into the kitchen. His nose immediately detected a smell, a good smell, one he hadn't smelled in a good long time.

Ohh...Simone had baked cookies.

Real cookies. Not horse cookies.

"Is that you?" Simone called from the other room.

"Don't know who else it would be," he called back. Simone appeared in the doorway to the kitchen.

"I smell 'em," he said. "Where'd you hide them?"

"I 'hid' them in the cookie jar."

"Smart," he said, wagging his finger at her. "Very smart. I woulda never looked there."

He opened the cookie jar and smiled.

"Shortbread cookies," Simone said. "You mentioned you like them. And they're easy to make— only three ingredients."

"No, you did a very nice job here," he said, popping a cookie in his mouth. It was all sugar, all butter, and all heaven.

She walked over to him and stole a cookie from the jar for herself.

"I'm playing house," she said. "My kitchen's the size of a closet, if that. It's much more fun to bake when you don't have to stand in the bathtub to reach the oven."

"I'll never understand why you New Yorkers spend so much money on such tiny little apartments."

"For the city," she said. "It has everything."

"Except good-sized kitchens."

"Except that," she said. "You have a good day at work, dear?" She grinned, playing house again.

"For the most part. Then it all went to hell in the last five minutes."

"What happened?" she asked, smile immediately gone. "The horses are okay, aren't they?"

It touched him she was worried about the horses.

"They're fine. It's just ah...Luke Bradley called. Said some things I didn't like to hear."

"Luke Bradley? Oh, yeah, the guy who was supposed to be Mister November. What's up with Luke?"

Jason didn't know how to tell her, or if he should, but he'd already started...

"I'm not one to gossip," Jason said.

"Yeah, I noticed," she said.

"But Luke called asking how the photoshoot went. And then he asked me if you were as sexy in person as you were in your pictures."

"Oh," she said, nodding. "He's been on my website, I guess. I have a few of my corset pics on there."

"Yup. He's been on it. A lot. He's a fan."

"That's nice of him to say."

Jason's eyes widened. Simone wasn't being sarcastic.

"Nice? What he was saying wasn't nice."

"Did my pics turn him on?"

"He might have implied that."

Simone leaned back on the counter, a cookie in her hands. She pointed it at him.

"You know when a grown woman engages in something called 'fetish photography'...she kind of expects some men—and women—will enjoy the view."

"It doesn't bother you?"

"It's sort of the point. And if you're a person like me

who doesn't think porn and masturbating are bad things—in moderation—then why would I be offended to know someone got turned on looking at my pictures? That's what they're for. If I wanted people to look at my photos and not get turned on, I would post pictures of forests and flowers, not my tits tied up in a corset. I do fetish photography for a reason. And that reason is, A —because it turns me on and makes me happy, and B —because it turns other people on and makes them happy. If they turned your friend Luke on, great. He's in the hospital, right? I hope I could distract him from being bored and in pain for a few minutes."

Jason took a deep long breath. "Damn," he said.

"What?"

"You are something else, Spanky. I almost feel like I should tell Luke I'm sorry for threatening to kill him over him perving on you. I'm not gonna, just to be clear. He was being a real ass. There is a way of talking about how pretty girls are without being as crude as he was. He's usually not that bad. I don't know. Maybe it was the painkillers."

"Posturing," Simone said, waving her hand dismissively.

"What?"

"He's a male submissive," Simone said. "And he's posturing to hide it."

Jason's jaw dropped to the floor and down into the basement.

"You're kidding me," he said. "Luke? He's the toughest guy I know."

"And the toughest guys I know regularly get the crap beaten out of them by the toughest women I know."

"You sure about this?" Jason asked, still skeptical.

"I wouldn't bet your farm on it, but I'm trained to figure this stuff out. When I talked to him on the phone when he was still our potential Mister November, he asked me if I was going to order him around during the shoot and make him do all kinds of crazy stuff. He acted like he was joking, but I could tell he kind of hoped that would happen. I almost told him that I have a dominatrix friend who takes referrals and would happily fly out to Montana to beat the hell out of a cowboy and make him lick her boots."

"I am going to tell him that. I might tell him that right now." Jason started to take his phone out of his pocket, but Simone stopped him by putting her arms around him and kissing him.

"Don't, please," she said. "He'll think you're making fun of him. We don't make fun of male submissives any more than we make fun of other kinky people for their kinks. Like male dominants who get very grumpy and possessive when other men talk about finding their slaves attractive. Which is very sexy," Simone said. "Not that it should be. But it is."

"I'm a big fan of your body," Jason said. "I just gotta be at peace with the fact that I'm not the only fan of it out there. It's none of my business. I'm going to keep telling myself that. None of my business at all." He took another deep breath, a cleansing breath.

"Feel better?" Simone asked.

"Not a damn bit."

She laughed, a bright bubbling laugh, like she had champagne in her soul. "I hate to tell you this, Jason, but there are a *whole* lot of sexy pics of you online, too. And I guarantee girls all over the country have stared at them and had the same kind of fantasies about you that men have about me."

"I was in Levi's ads and truck ads. Girls do not get like *that* over truck ads."

"Girls do get like *that* over sexy cowboys in tight jeans with great smiles who win lots of trophies. There's even a whole Tumblr devoted to your a... derrière. I found it this morning. It's called 'Jason Waters & His Chaps of Glory,' and if you think I'm making that up, we're getting on Twitter right now and clicking the hashtag #chapsofglory."

"You are kidding me," he said. He didn't know whether to laugh or cry. The Chaps of Glory? Seriously?

"Yep. At least two hundred gifs of you riding horses and bulls in slow motion. I counted because I have saved every last one of them to my hard drive."

"That is totally different," he said. He had his clothes on in those photographs, after all.

"You keep telling yourself that, sir," she said,

shaking her head and smiling. "But I know you are one sexy cowboy, and I'm not the only woman in the country who has noticed."

He narrowed his eyes at her. "The Chaps of Glory?" he said, taking her sweet ass into his hands. "I'm never going online again."

"Pages of pictures, Jason. Screenshots. Your Levi's ads. iPhone pics from girls who followed you around at rodeo events just to get pictures of you from behind."

"I was wondering what the hell those girls were doing back there," he said. "Thought I'd split my pants."

"Now you know. Do you feel better?" she asked.

"I feel mighty flattered. I didn't know my ass was that good."

"I'm a fangirl of it," Simone said. "You want to see the Tumblr?"

"Never in a billion years," he said.

"Fine. I'll just go back to watching your YouTube videos like I've been doing all day," she said.

"Oh Lord, how bored were you today?"

"I might have fallen down the Jason 'Still' Waters Google hole. I have to admit, it's sexy watching you ride."

"You see my wreck?"

"No, is that on there?" she asked.

"Might not be anymore. It gets taken down a lot since it's not very pretty. I have it, though, somewhere on my computer if you want to see why I quit the business."

"I admit I'm curious," she said.

He took Simone into his office and fired up his computer. Took him only a few seconds to find the video.

"You really want to watch this?" Simone asked.

"I've seen it a dozen times. It's pretty wild. I watch it and don't even feel like it's me, you know."

With a few clicks, he pulled up the video. There he was in the chute, on the back of a bull called Demented, a legendary cowboy killer. He watched himself cinch his bull rope. Not once did he look at the camera. He hadn't even known it was there. In that moment, in that zone, that place of cold zero and absolute concentration, no one existed but him and the bull. Then the gate flew open and they were out in the arena.

"There's a vest we wear," Jason said, "practically bulletproof. Protects your chest and back. They invented it after Lane Frost got killed in '89. But this son of a bitch got his horn under the edge of the vest and just let it rip."

In the video it happened so fast that only slo-mo revealed the sequence of events. As the slow-motion replay began, Jason watched himself make it eight seconds on the back of Demented before getting thrown off the moment the horn blew. Demented whirled on him, spinning on a dime, which a twenty-five-hundred-pound animal shouldn't be able to do. The horned head went down and hit Jason in the hip; the horn slipped under the vest and Jason watched as he was flipped ten feet in the air. When he landed, half his side was torn open.

The video ended.

"The good thing," Jason said, "is that even with the horn under the vest, that vest kept it from being a helluva lot worse than it was. You want to see it again? I can never believe how high he tosses me. I look like a damn rag doll."

Simone didn't say anything. Jason turned and saw her standing behind his desk chair with tears running down her face.

"Baby, I'm sorry," he said. "I didn't mean to scare you."

"I'm not scared," she said. "I'm just...I'm so glad you're alive."

He reached for her without saying another word and pulled her into his lap. She wrapped her arms around his neck and clung to him.

"I'm a damn fool. I shouldn't have shown that to you," he said. "I just didn't want you thinking it was all, you know, chaps of glory."

"You really thought you were crazy because you like kink?" she asked. "Kink is not crazy. Bull riding is fucking crazy."

Jason laughed softly and didn't even scold her for swearing. She might have a point there.

"It paid the bills," he said.

"So does literally every other job that doesn't involve riding angry bulls with giant horns."

"I wouldn't make much of an accountant," he said.

Simone sighed and shook her head. "At least you retired while you could still walk," she said. "And fuck."

"You are really pushing it, Spanky."

"Sorry, sir," she said, sounding almost genuinely contrite. "I got a little freaked out there. You could have died."

"I could have died, yeah."

"And I never would have met you."

"Would that have been so bad?" he asked. "We only met twenty-four hours ago."

"True," she said. "But it's been such a good twenty-four hours."

He didn't argue with that. He might even say it was about the best twenty-four hours of his life. He'd pursued his bull riding career with focus and determination, and as much as he'd relished the challenges and enjoyed the victories, his injury, bad as it was, had almost come as a relief. Now he had a reason to walk away with his head held high. But there'd been no joy in bull riding for him. Pleasure, yes? No twenty-something guy hated getting all the female attention and adulation he'd received. But real happiness? *That* was this morning, getting a pony ready for a brave little girl. Happiness was holding Simone in his arms when she lost her footing after jumping out of the saddle. It was right now with her in his arms, wiping her tears on his dirty shirt because she'd been heartbroken to see him getting hurt. And it was last night with her on her knees in front of him, calling him "sir" and making every last one of his most private fantasies come true.

"All right, enough crying now," he said. "You're gonna make me feel bad for showing you my video."

"Don't feel bad," she said. "I'm glad I saw it. I want to know you better, and that was a big moment in your past."

"All in the past," he said. "Old news. I only showed it to you because I was trying to impress you. Did it work?"

"No," she said, and he swatted her ass. "Only because you already impressed me so much that nothing else you could do would impress me any more."

"That's a big statement," he said.

"I should be the one trying to impress you," she said.

"You got any bull riding videos?" he asked.

"Nope, but I got videos. Want to see one?" She sat back and grinned wickedly at him. He wasn't sure he trusted that smile.

"I don't know. Do I?"

"I think you do."

"All right. Now you got me curious."

Simone put her foot on the floor and spun his

swivel chair around so she could reach his keyboard while remaining on his lap. And that was fine by him. She could leave that sweet ass of hers on his thighs all day and all night.

"This is stuff your friend Luke is not going to see online. It's on my private Kinklife page. Only a few people have access to it."

"Kinklife?"

"Yeah, I'd highly suggest clearing your browser history before your sister comes to visit again," she said.

"Good Lord."

She tapped rapidly on the keys and in a few seconds she'd pulled up a video of her own.

"You know what Florentine flogging is?" Simone asked him.

"New one on me."

"That's when you flog with two floggers at once," she said. "One in each hand. It comes from a style of fencing where the fencers fight with two swords at once. It's pretty hard to do, apparently. I've never tried it, but this is me on the receiving end. What do you think?"

Simone hit play on the video and Jason leaned in to watch.

"I think..." he breathed, "I think I like your video better than mine is what I think."

13

Simone wasn't trying to show off or anything—not really, well, maybe a little bit—but she desperately wanted to get the image of Jason being tossed around by a giant angry bull out of her head. What better way than watching some playful kink to clear their heads? And maybe Jason would get over his fear of hurting her if he could see the sort of S&M she did on a regular basis. The video she showed him was a few years old, filmed back when she still had her rainbow-striped hair, but she'd kept it up on her profile because it had been such a fun night at her club.

"So that's Mistress Nora," she said to Jason when a beautiful black-haired woman in a red corset and back carnival mask turned and smiled provocatively at the camera. "She's my friend I texted about you earlier."

"Pretty lady," he said. "Not my type, though."

"What's wrong?"

"Hair's not pink enough."

Simone grinned. "And that naked girl is obviously me."

"Yes, I can see that," he said. "Does your momma know you do this online?"

"My videos are all private. You have to get my permission to view my page. And even if Mom did see them, what can I say? You go to a website called Kinklife, you're going to see kink. Not my problem if someone goes looking for trouble and finds it."

Simone pointed at the scene again. "That's one of the dungeons at the club I work at sometimes."

Jason leaned in to get a closer look at the screen. Simone was pleased by the look of rapt attention on his face.

"What's that?" he asked pointing at the screen.

"That's a St. Andrew's Cross," she said. "You tie people to it and flog them or cane them or whatever."

"You get those with Amazon Prime?" he asked.

"Never looked. I wouldn't be surprised if you could, though."

"Who's doing the filming?" Jason asked.

"Mr. King. My boss," she said. "Or he was before he retired and moved to New Orleans."

Simone studied Jason as he watched Mistress Nora cuff Simone's wrists high up on the cross. Then she picked up her floggers—one red and one black—and began a light flogging up and down Simone's entire backside from her calves to her shoulders.

"Nice," Jason said and she could tell he meant it. He'd lifted up the back of her shirt and his hands drifted sensually over her lower back and sides. "You in the habit of making movies?" he asked.

"Not really," she said. "But we did sometimes on request. This was for a very important client of Mistress Nora's. He loves FemDom/femsub."

"And that is?"

"Female dominant, female submissive."

"I can see the appeal," he said. "You and your friend Nora seem pretty cozy."

Jason said that as Nora, in the video, ran her hand over Simone's body—her back, her front, her breasts, and even between her legs.

"She and I were...um...*close,*" Simone said. "We played together a lot."

"You like women?" Jason asked.

"I'm very attracted to dominance," Simone admitted. "Dominant men and dominant women. I don't have crushes on women as a rule but when she's a dominant and a sadist like Mistress Nora, I get a little gooey. That bother you?"

"Bother me? That you been with a woman? Hot and bother maybe."

Simone laughed. "When a beautiful woman tells you she wants to tie you to her bed and force you to have orgasms until you faint, what are you going to do? Say no?"

"I'd be hard-pressed to decline that offer myself," Jason said.

"The good Mistress has very talented hands," Simone said.

"She's pretty tough with those floggers, too," Jason said.

"Nora doesn't pull her punches, that's for sure," Simone said. "Not that I'd want her to. I know it's hard for people to understand why submissive masochists like what they like, but there's just something incredibly sexy to me about submitting to someone dominant and powerful. Mistress Nora could have ordered me to clean her dungeon or polish her boots and I would have loved it. But the beatings are even more fun and special. It's very intimate to let someone hurt you. And then there are the marks on you afterwards. They're like prizes."

"Prizes?"

"You ever make out with somebody super sexy and end up with swollen lips and a hickey on your neck the next day?"

"Once or twice," Jason said.

"Did you like it?" she asked. "Having a little love bite on your body to remind you of how much fun you had when you got it?"

"Been there," Jason said.

"The marks on a submissive from a beating are the

same thing," she said. "Only times a hundred. Or a thousand."

Simone was glad to see Jason nod, and she hoped he was starting to truly understand her love of pain and dominance. She didn't want him hating himself every time he left a mark on her while they were playing. She wanted him to find the welts and bruises he left on her as sexy as she did.

Back in the video clip, Mistress Nora was in full-flogging mode, striking Simone over and over again from her ankles to her shoulders.

"You can see she skips over my kidney area," Simone said. "You don't want to play hard around there."

"Makes sense," Jason said, still staring at the screen. "How much does that hurt?"

"The pain from a flogging really depends on a lot of things," Simone said. "Certain types of floggers will hurt worse than others. If the falls are narrow—"

"The what?"

"The tails," she said. "Those dangling leather things on a flogger. They're either tails or falls. If the falls are narrow, they'll sting. If they're wide, they'll thud. And the sensation also depends on how the flogger is being used. In Florentine flogging, it feels like you're being slapped over and over. When the flogger is thrown..." Simone held up her hands and demonstrated how to hold the tips of the tails and snap them, "that can really sting. It can even break the skin if the thrower has a good arm and good aim. So for you, maybe you should think about learning to Florentine? Since you don't like breaking the skin. Or a deer-skin flogger. You can put a lot of power into it and you probably won't break the skin."

"I like the sound of that," Jason said. "What's she using?"

"Not sure what the material is. But those are narrow falls, probably oiled leather, so they sting like fire ants. Mister S, her master, he uses buffalo floggers a lot. You have to be insanely strong to use buffalo. It's big, it's heavy and it packs a wallop."

"How big a wallop?"

Simone paused the video and pulled up a photograph on her profile. A picture of her, naked, kneeling on the floor in front of the fireplace at Mr. King's Manhattan townhouse.

"You see those black and blue bruises up and down my back?" Simone asked. "That was the day after a scene with Mister S and his buffalo flogger."

"Hmm..." was all Jason said.

"It's fun," she said. "And I heal fast."

"That's a lot of bruises," he said. "You really liked that?"

"With him? Yes," she said. "When you really respect your master, the bruises he gives you during a scene feel like badges of honor. That's why I like taking pictures of my bruises and saving them. But only the really good ones."

She flipped back to the video where Nora was flogging her with a new flogger, brown leather and thuddy.

"That's her elk flogger. It's good for a cool-down flogging. Little bit softer."

"What's that?" He pointed at her feet in the video.

"That's called a spreader bar," Simone said. "It's an adjustable metal bar, and you attach it to cuffs with hooks. That way I can't close my legs."

"Can't close your legs?"

"Not even if I tried," she said.

"I need to start a shopping list," Jason said. "We're gonna need half a dozen of those, a St. Andrew's cross, ten or twelve sets of floggers. Where's my credit card?"

Simone grinned before remembering she'd be long gone out of Jason's life by the time any kinky shipments started arriving.

"I have some of this stuff at home," she said. "Wish I'd packed my toy bag. I have floggers in it, a spreader bar, cuffs and stuff."

"If you're the submissive, why do you have floggers?"

"I like having my own set of gear," she said. "That way it's there if I have a kinky friend come over, and we decide to play."

"Play? That what you all call it?" He sounded doubtful.

"It's fun, you know? Play time. Mr. King even calls his dungeon his 'playroom.'"

"You feel like you're playing with me?" he asked.

Simone shut off the video and shifted on his lap to face him.

"Yes and no," she said.

"What do you mean?"

"Well, yes, because it's fun, like I said. No because it's...I don't know. More than that," she said. "What about you? Do you feel like we're playing?"

"Sometimes," he said. "Sometimes it feels, I don't know, kind of real."

"When does it feel real?" she asked.

"When you're being my little slave," he said. "When you're on your knees or I'm spanking you and you're squealing on my lap. And when I'm inside you...it doesn't seem like it's play then. It seems like you're really into it. And I know I am. But maybe you're a real good actress?"

"I'm not acting, Jason. While I'm here with you until I leave, I'm yours. For real. When you give me an order, I obey it. I want to obey it."

He touched her forehead with his fingertips, ran his fingers through her hair. Simone shivered at the tender touch. The look in his eyes was inscrutable. She would have given anything to know what he was thinking.

"Does that scare you?" she asked.

"A little," he said and it meant more than she could say that he was willing to admit that. "Scares me how good it feels, too. What if I can't go back to being with a girl who isn't like you?"

"Why would you want to?" she asked, giving him a little smile.

"Well, considering you don't live here, and I don't plan on spending the rest of my life sleeping alone..."

"Fair," she conceded. "Still, a lot of women are very open-minded if you give them a chance."

"I can't imagine telling anyone the things I've told you about me."

"I know it takes a lot of trust."

"You've spoiled me," Jason said. "You already know everything and I know nothing. If I met a girl and she was as ignorant about this stuff as I was, I don't think we'd get very far."

"You'd figure it out," Simone said. "All couples have to, kinky or vanilla."

"Maybe I oughta just tie you to my bed and not let you ever leave."

"I've heard worse ideas."

Simone and Jason met eyes. She wanted to believe he wasn't joking. She wanted to believe he wanted her to stay. Not that she could, of course. Or could she?

No point even answering that question until he asked it.

"You want to see some more of my pictures?" she asked.

"More than I want to breathe and eat and sleep," he said.

Simone giggled happily as she turned back to his computer and pulled up more of her photographs.

Jason rested his chin on her shoulder and wrapped his arms around her waist as she showed him pictures she'd taken of her kinky friends, pictures of her posing in various submissive positions, and a few normal vanilla, i.e. clothed, pictures of her out and about in the Big Apple.

"You have a nice life in New York," he said after she showed him a photo of her and her friend Tessa—another submissive at their club—dressed up to see *Hamilton*. A client of Tessa's had given her tickets.

"It has perks," Simone said. "And its downsides. Like anywhere you live."

"Never heard a New Yorker yet tell me what they don't like about the town. It's nothing but the greatest city in the world, best place to live, nothing like it... What don't you like about it?"

"Oh, the usual," she said, shifting to face him. "It's kind of loud at night. Rents are high. You're not there."

He raised his eyebrow at her. "And that's a downside?" he asked.

"I'll definitely miss you when I go back," she said.

"You gonna post pictures of me on your secret page?" he asked. "Something to remember me by?"

"No," she said, rolling her eyes. "You have kids who write you fan letters, remember? This is all top secret."

Jason stared at her a few seconds before leaning forward and pulling up the picture of her kneeling in front of the fireplace again, the one that showed off the bruises on her back.

"Who took that picture?" Jason asked.

"Self-portrait. I was experimenting with lighting," she said. The photo had turned out well. She looked like a real fetish model in it.

"I was looking more at the curves than the lighting."

"Not the bruises?"

"I'm trying to pretend I left those on you and not some other man."

"You could leave bruises on me," she said. "I'd like that."

"And I like the thought of you taking pictures of the marks I leave on you," he said. "Like that." He pointed at the screen.

"They fade so fast, if you want to preserve them, photography is the best way to do it."

"Will you take some pictures of yourself?" he asked. "Private ones just for me?"

"Are you ordering me to?" she asked, grinning.

"I suppose I am."

"I will definitely obey that order, sir."

"I suppose I better put some marks on you first."

"I suppose you better, Master Jason," she said.

She loved the way Jason was looking at her right now, like a lost man looks when he stumbles out of the forest after days of wandering and sees the road that'll lead him home. She wanted to be that path for him. But she wanted to be there when he got home, too. Too much to ask? Maybe. But maybe not.

Jason wrapped his hand around the back of her neck and pulled her to him—gently—and then kissed her—not gently. The kiss was so not gentle that Simone nearly slid off Jason's lap. He caught her at the last second, and they both laughed.

"Whew," she said. "You know it's a good kiss when you almost fall out of your chair."

"I got you, Spanky," he said, pulling her closer and tighter to him.

Oh, yeah, he definitely had her. He kissed her again, a long kiss that neither one of them seemed willing to end. Minutes passed and they kept kissing. In the back of her mind, Simone vaguely wondered when was the last time she simply sat in a man's lap and made out with him. She couldn't remember. If Jason kept kissing her like that she wouldn't remember her own name by the time he was through with her. He pulled her hair off her neck and pressed his lips against her throat. She moaned at the tug of his teeth on the thin, tender skin, moaned again as his tongue lapped at the little wound he'd made by biting her there.

"There," he said into her ear. "That's gonna leave a bruise."

"I'll be sure to take a picture of it for you, sir," she said. "And maybe one for me, too. Tomorrow, after they turn into nice bruises."

"Tomorrow? What should we do tonight then?"

Simone glanced around the room, looking for

inspiration. She found it sitting right in front of her on Jason's desk. His laptop still had her flogging video pulled up.

"Do you want to make a video, sir?"

That raised his eyebrow.

"That a yes?" she asked.

Jason set her on her feet and stood up. Then he took her by the wrist and pulled her out of the office and up the stairs.

It was a "yes."

14

Jason took Simone into the guest room again, sat her on the edge of the bed and stood in front of her, his hands on her face, his thumbs stroking her cheeks.

"You sure about this?" she asked. He didn't blame her for asking that, as unsure as he was most of the time.

"If it's too much, we'll turn the camera off," he said. "What do you need?"

"My camera equipment's in your room in the black bag. I'll need to set up the camera on the tripod. After that...it's up to you, sir."

"I want you in your corset," he said.

"I better get it then," she said. "I'll need you to lace me in good and tight, sir, if you will."

"Oh, I will." He loved the way she was looking at him. She looked so sweet and trusting, a little lamb to the slaughter. "And I'll fuck your pussy, too. And anything else I want to fuck."

Her lips parted and she breathed a heavy breath.

"My body belongs to you," she said. "Every inch."

It could have been a line, Simone acting the part. But he didn't think so, not with the way her breath caught in her throat. He touched the bright red bite mark he'd left on her neck then dropped his head to kiss it again. He cupped her breast in his hand while he kissed her and felt her nipple harden against his palm through her t-shirt.

He was hard, too, had been since the second he'd sunk his teeth into her skin downstairs and heard her moan in his ear. What was he going to do with himself after she was gone, and he came home to an empty house? It hurt too much to imagine. He forced the thought from his mind.

"Go get your things," he said. "And make it quick. Don't make me wait for you."

"Yes, sir," she said, breathlessly. He swatted her ass when she moved past him.

"Spanky?"

"Yes, sir?" She turned around in the doorway when he called for her.

"Bring me my crop from the bedroom, too."

She grinned ear to ear. "Yes, sir."

After she left, Jason stared at the bed and wondered what on earth was possessing him to do this. Make a video of himself having sex with Simone?

What was he going to do with it? Watch it, of course. Watch it every day and every night after she'd gone. If he couldn't have her, this would be the next best thing.

She returned quickly, bag in one hand, corset in the other, crop between her teeth. He laughed at the sight of her, so obedient to his "make it quick" command that she'd found a way to bring everything into the room in one trip.

Pretty damn adorable if you asked him.

Simone dropped her corset onto the bed, set the camera bag on the floor and with a curtsey presented him his crop.

"Nice," he said. She smiled as she went to work. He liked watching a competent woman at her work. As easy as one, two, three, she'd unzipped her bag, set up her tripod, set up her camera, and had it aimed and ready to go.

"All set?" he asked.

"Just have to turn it on. Whenever you're ready, sir."

He looked at the corset she'd laid on the bed—pale pink with black laces. Soon she'd be wearing that and nothing else, and he'd be pulling the laces tight, tighter, tightest...And it was all going to be on camera for him to look at and enjoy anytime he wanted.

"I'm ready," he said.

Simone hit a few buttons on the camera and then stood up, facing him, waiting.

He picked up her corset and waited. She got the

hint. Stepping in front of the camera by the bed, Simone began to undress. She didn't do it slowly. She didn't do it quickly. But she did undress gracefully, putting on a good show for the camera and for him.

When she was completely naked he went to her, corset in hand. She sat on the bed and raised her arms over her head. He slipped the corset down her arms. He let her adjust things here and there a moment before she stood up with her back to him.

Time to tighten the laces. He willed his hands not to shake for the camera when he reached out and stroked her back. The corset was satiny and warm from the heat of her skin. It had stiff ribs in it—*stays* he thought they were called—and a black lace trim around the top and bottom edges. The best part was... the corset would only cover her from hip to right under her breasts. He wanted nothing between him and her beautiful nipples.

He turned her sideways so that the camera could catch him tightening her laces. Why he found the idea so erotic, he didn't know. Maybe because it was a way for him to take power over her body. Maybe because it was like tying her up. Maybe because he had a fetish for all things pink and lacy and frilly on a beautiful curvy woman. Whatever the reason, Jason didn't want to rush a thing. He started right below her shoulder blades and slipped one finger under the laces, pulling them out six inches from her skin. The two halves of the corset slid closer together. Simone raised her arms again and rested them crossed over her head. He pulled tighter and the two halves of the corset met. And when they did he leaned forward and kissed her naked shoulder. The kiss became a bite when he drew a nip of her skin between his teeth and sucked on it. Simone gasped and he nearly stopped at once before remembering that, not only was he allowed to bite her and mark her and make her gasp, she wanted him to do it. She'd asked him to do it. And for this girl, he'd do anything. Apart from the corset, Simone was naked. No panties between him and her beautiful backside and her pussy, which he was dying to stroke. He made himself wait because that meant Simone had to wait, too.

Jason was pleased to see he'd left a good-sized mark on her shoulder. A pretty red welt. He touched it, kissed it, licked it.

"Does it hurt?" he asked her.

"It throbs a little, sir," she said.

"Red, wet, and throbbing," he said into her ear. "That's how I want your pussy."

"Keep doing what you're doing, sir, and you'll get it."

Jason had every intention of doing just that. He dug his hands under the next rung of laces and yanked, hard. Simone gasped again, and he mockingly laughed in her ear. He couldn't recall a time when he'd felt this good with a woman. In control. Respected. Wanted. He never wanted it to end.

Dangerous thought, right? God knew he adored the hell out of this girl already. Too fast. Too soon. He should be scared to death. But he wasn't. For the first time in a long time, and even with a camera on him, he was doing exactly what he wanted to be doing. No guilt. No shame. And nobody's goddamn business but his and Simone's.

He yanked the next rung of laces. It was all for show. He wasn't pulling them very tight. Last thing he wanted was Simone to pass out on him before he could have his way with her. But he sure was having a ball acting like he was going to lace her up tight enough to squeeze the air out of her lungs. He could tell from her hard breathing that her lungs were working just fine.

As he laced his way down to her waist, he let himself pull in a little tighter and soon Simone's hourglass figure was dramatically showcased in pink satin and black lace. He tied a bow at the end and placed his hands on her narrow waist, relishing how it flared out to her round hips and up to her full breasts. He slid his hands to the front of the corset, placing them flat against her stomach, and pulled her back against him. Her head fell back against his chest, and she made a soft sound of arousal and surrender.

"Mine," he whispered. A smile danced across her face. He slid his hands up to her bare breasts, holding them firmly, possessively. "Mine," he said again.

He moved low, cupping his hand between her thighs. She was hot, and when he pushed his middle finger through her slit, he found she was wet, too. His cock ached to get into that wet hole, but he didn't want to rush it. He'd just gotten started playing with her body.

Jason didn't tell her to lie on her back on the bed. He put her on her back on the bed. She went without protest, putty in his hands. When he had her where he wanted her, he yanked off his shirt, stripped out of his jeans and boxer briefs and, completely forgetting the camera was on him, straddled Simone across her waist. He took her wrists in his hands and pinned them over her head while he pressed his mouth to her mouth, his tongue against her tongue and his cock against her corset.

Simone returned the kiss with equal intensity. She opened her mouth for him, rubbed her tongue against his, arched underneath him to press more of her body against his. She might have been a submissive, and she was definitely his little slave, but she wasn't passive, and she certainly wasn't meek. Jason kissed her neck, her chest and then her breasts. He took a nipple in his mouth and sucked deeply, relishing the moan that Simone released. He held her breast in his hand and sucked the nipple even harder. Carefully he pressed his teeth against the tender pink areola and sucked again, leaving another deliberate love bite that she could take a picture of tomorrow when it had turned into a purple bruise. Simone flinched when he dug his teeth in and he had to remind himself again that a flinch of pain didn't mean he needed to stop. It seemed too good to be true almost, that he'd stumbled across a woman who loved being treated like his personal sexual property. He'd been so resigned to keeping his fantasies as fantasies. He felt like a kid who asked for a bicycle for Christmas when he really wanted a Porsche, never requesting his real desire because he knew for a fact it was a waste of a wish. But here she was...underneath him, warm, beautiful, wet and waiting for his cock and loving every wicked thing he did to her as much as he loved doing it.

"You are too good to be true," he whispered against her skin.

"That's funny, sir," she said.

"And why's that?" he asked.

"I keep thinking the same thing about you."

He smiled up at her and knew he was just about as happy as he'd ever been or would ever be. That feeling only grew as he left bite marks all over Simone's body. One on her shoulder. One on her chest. One on her thigh. One on her hip. She writhed and giggled as he licked and sucked and nibbled all over her. As he sucked on her nipples again, Simone lifted her hips up against his cock.

"You want to be fucked, don't you?" he asked.

"Need's the word," she said. "Sir."

"Well, I might like to get a little rough with you," he said, "but I wouldn't want to torture you. Don't want to torture myself either."

But maybe he did want to torture her—a little bit, anyway. He straddled her chest again and took her breasts into his hands. He pushed them together and thrust his cock between them. Her skin was smooth and hot against his cock and he nearly came all over her chest from that first thrust alone. He made himself calm down, if only so he wouldn't embarrass himself. But it wasn't easy. Simone arched her back underneath him again, offering her breasts to him. He held them firmly in his hands, squeezing as he rubbed his erection all over them. Simone closed her eyes and her head fell back on the bed in total surrender.

"There's nothing I can't do to you, is there?" he asked.

"Nothing," she breathed.

"I could fuck every inch of your body and you'd want it."

"I want it," she said.

"I could tie you to the bed and leave you there the rest of your life."

"I could live in your bed the rest of my life," she said. "As long as you keep doing that."

That was Jason rubbing her nipples over and over with his thumbs. They were hard and bright red from how hard he'd sucked them. He smiled when he remembered they were on camera now, and he'd get to see them whenever he wanted. But what he wanted right that second was to fuck her, the sooner the better.

Jason moved off her and issued an order. "Turn over."

Simone obeyed at once. She knelt on her elbows and her knees. Jason got behind her and eyed the view. "Hope the camera's getting this," he said as he opened her pussy with his fingers and stroked her inner folds.

"I can take pictures of my pussy for you, sir," she said.

"You should probably do that then," he said. "A whole goddamned album of your pussy."

He put a finger inside her and his eyes rolled back in his head at the feel of her wet, hot, silky vagina. He stroked her with two fingers, long strokes all the way into her and out again. She groaned in pleasure and opened her legs even wider for him.

"That an invitation?" he asked.

"You don't need one, sir."

"That's right, I don't. A man doesn't need an engraved invitation to come in his own house."

He grabbed the condoms off the bedside table and when he had one on, he rose up on his knees and pressed the head against her entrance. With a slow hard thrust he pushed into her and with a second harder thrust he sheathed himself all the way inside.

Jason had never seen a sexier sight than his own big roughed-up hands wrapped around her narrow waist encased in her pink corset. He took control of her body, pulling her back against him when he wanted to go deep, pushing her away as he pulled out. He loved seeing his cock disappear inside her and then reappear a moment later, slick with her wetness. He wanted to come but he thought he ought to slow down and wait for her sake. Then he remembered she was his to do with as he pleased, and if he wanted to come right then and there he would come, right then and right there.

Jason thrust into her faster, then harder, then faster and harder. He pounded her from behind and she panted and grunted and groaned as he let go and gave her everything he had to give. Her cries mixed with his own as his orgasm built to a fever pitch. When he came it was so intense he thought he was going to black out from sheer pleasure. The muscle spasms were deep, reaching all the way into his back. As the climax crested and faded, Jason hung over Simone's back, still gripping her waist and breathing until he was in control of himself again.

He pulled out of her and rolled up the condom in the wrapper. The entire time Simone stayed on her knees, awaiting his next order. He grabbed her around the waist and pulled her down and back against his chest.

"Touch yourself," he said as he wrapped his arms around her and took her breasts in his hands again. "Make yourself come for me."

She didn't hesitate, his sexy, sweet and utterly shameless little slave. She moved her hand between her legs and found her clitoris with her fingertips. She rubbed it and he watched the show, and if he hadn't come a minute earlier he would have been rock hard. Simone dipped her middle finger inside herself and then spread her own wetness over her clitoris. As she stroked it, she moved her hips in slow circles. Jason massaged her breasts and whispered encouragement in her ear. *You're so sexy...so fucking sexy...so beautiful... come for me, baby girl...I want to hear you come...*

In no time she was panting again, gasping and groaning. Her hips rose off the bed and she let out a hoarse cry. He held her through her climax and held her after she finished and collapsed back against him.

"God damn," Jason said with a long breath.

"You took the words right out of my mouth," she said then giggled, wiggling around to lay her head on his chest.

"How do you know exactly what to do to make me feel so good?"

"I don't know," Simone said. "Just glad I do."

He stroked her back with his fingertips, happy to simply hold her and touch her. And he better do it, too, hold her and touch her as much as he could, since she would be leaving soon. Unless he ordered her to stay. No, he couldn't do that. You couldn't order someone to stay with you, could you? That wouldn't be right. He couldn't force Simone into staying with him. That wasn't fair to her. But he could ask her to stay, couldn't he? Maybe he could. Maybe he would. Maybe he'd never get invited home for Christmas again, either.

It shouldn't be this hard to fall in love with someone.

"Master Jason..."

"Yes, Spanky?"

"Nothing. I just like saying that."

He kissed the top of her head.

Maybe it wasn't so hard to fall in love after all.

15

Simone spent the next morning wandering around Jason's house in a sort of daze. They'd had sex as soon as he'd woken up, but he'd let her stay in bed afterwards to sleep some more while he'd gone out to check on the horses.

He was out there now. Every few minutes she'd peek out the west-facing window and see him in the paddock with one horse or another. She wished she'd brought the telephoto lens for her camera. She would have loved to get some shots of him with his horses to keep with her after she left.

Tomorrow.

She left tomorrow. And not tomorrow evening or tomorrow afternoon, but tomorrow morning. And she was definitely leaving. She had to go. She had a packed schedule the next two weeks. A christening. A Sweet Sixteen party being thrown for the daughter of a New

York district attorney. A big wedding in the Hamptons and then another wedding reception to shoot next weekend, which she could not miss for anything in the world since she knew the couple. She couldn't back out of all her commitments just because she'd met a guy.

So she had to leave.

Unless Jason ordered her to stay?

No, he wouldn't do that. He respected her too much to make her miss work. The last thing Simone wanted was for things to end badly with Jason. She was his first kink partner and that was a big deal for anyone. One bad early experience could turn someone off for life. She wanted him to look back on their week together with pleasure, not anger, frustration, or shame. She wanted to leave him with nothing but good memories. He'd been a wonderful master—possessive but understanding, tough but fair, playful even as he punished, and so sexy she was certain she'd never find a man who could compete with him. After her shower that morning she'd stood naked in front of the bathroom mirror, admiring the black and blue bite marks he'd left all over her. An even dozen. She'd counted.

She sighed another deep sigh as she stood at the window watching while Jason and Rusty trotted the paddock with one of the horses being trained for trail work. She was wrong. She'd thought the last thing she wanted was for things to end badly between them. The truth was, the last thing Simone wanted was for things to end between them, *period*.

Simone collapsed onto Jason's bed, which she'd made that morning after finally getting up. Such a comfortable bed, she could live and die in it. Or could she? Really? Could she, New Englander born and New Yorker bred, really live happily on a Kentucky horse farm with the nearest town—its population roughly equal to one city block of Brooklyn—half an hour away?

An image from the morning flashed across her mind—Jason on top of her, his mouth at her ear as he described in impressive detail just how good her pussy felt wrapped around his cock.

Yes, she decided. Yes, she could.

Simone sat up straight. "No," she told herself and then slapped the back of her left hand with her right hand. "Bad girl. Sane women do not fall in love with random cowboys after spending only four days with them."

Or did they?

Simone found her phone and sent a quick text message to her Mistress Nora. If anyone could put Simone's head on straight about Jason it was Nora.

"Do sane women fall in love with random cowboys after spending only four days with them?" Simone asked Nora.

She waited.

A few seconds later a reply appeared.

"Depends on the cowboy," Nora said.

"He trussed me up in a corset last night and fucked me—on camera."

"Marry him," Nora replied.

"You're supposed to tell me 'no,'" Simone replied.

Even though it was a text message, Simone could sense that Nora was sighing somewhere. She waited tensely for the reply.

"I have fallen in love at first sight," Nora wrote. "I have fallen in love slowly over a period of weeks and months. They both ended the same way—with me having ungodly amounts of kinky sex. There is no right way to fall in love. If he's happy and you're happy, that's all that matters."

"I'm not in love with him," Simone said. "I just keep thinking about how nice it would be to spend the rest of my life with him and be his cookie-baking slave forever. That wasn't a euphemism. I baked him cookies and he loved them and it made me happier than it should have. Also, he smells really good. And he spanks like a god. And he bought a therapy horse for a little girl who has speech problems after brain surgery. And I keep almost crying every time I think about leaving because I want to spend the rest of my life with him. That's not love, right?"

Nora replied with an emoji—a face with staring eyes and a straight line for a mouth. It was the one you sent when someone said something so patently foolish all you could do is stare at them in silence.

"Okay, so maybe I'm in love with him," Simone replied. "HELP!"

"You're in his house. He's fucking you constantly. Seems like you have it under control."

"I have to leave tomorrow morning," Simone told her.

"Good. Absence makes the cock grow harder, or whatever that saying is."

"But I'll miss him."

"You'll survive."

"I'm not sure I will. He's the best master I ever had."

"I'm telling you-know-who you said that."

Simone giggled.

"Doesn't count. Mister S and I never..."

"Poor you. He's very good at..."

"Nora, please, help me."

A long pause followed. As did a "..." which meant Nora was typing her message. Simone waited with baited breath.

The message finally arrived.

"You're smart. You're capable. You're 29 years old. Translation—you're on your own."

Simone nearly threw the phone across the room before she remembered it was an expensive phone and this was not her room.

Well, she couldn't blame Nora for not wanting to get involved. Simone was an adult woman. Jason was an adult man. They really should be able to figure things out together. And they would. Jason had proven to her already that he was a good man with a good head on his shoulders and an even better heart. She had to trust that if he wanted to see her again, he would say something to her. Wouldn't he?

She had to believe he would. He was the master in the relationship after all. She had to let him take the lead. Even though it was torture.

"You like torture," she reminded herself.

Not this kind of torture.

Desperate to take her mind off leaving in the morning, Simone decided to go ahead and take the photos Jason had requested of her. She could spend all day on that if she wanted. She could set up her backdrop, her lights, her timer, and make a really fancy digital photo album for him. That way after she was gone, he'd have the pictures to look at and remember how good they were together, which would then, of course, compel him to fly all the way to New York to tell her he was madly in love with her, then propose marriage, then throw her over his shoulder and carry her all the way back to Kentucky.

That last part might be a little farfetched, she knew. And maybe the marriage proposal. That might be a bit too sudden. They should probably know each other for at least a week before getting engaged.

But it was worth a try anyway.

With nothing else to do except pine for a man she hadn't even left yet, Simone went to work setting up a little photo studio in Jason's spare bedroom. She slipped out of her clothes and into her corset again. She couldn't get it quite as tight as Jason had but at least it would look nice in the pictures.

After two hours Simone had a few dozen very nice photographs of all her love bites plus a few bonus photos for Jason's eyes only. She threw her jeans and t-shirt back on and borrowed a flannel shirt of Jason's to wear for an extra layer of warmth. It was barely lunchtime, and it would probably be a few more hours before Jason finished with the horses. She wanted to help, but she also didn't want to get in his way. He'd asked her to come out around four to take another long ride with Cupcake. But what was she going to do until then?

She returned to the spare room to tear down her makeshift photo studio, but paused when an idea occurred to her.

Hadn't Jason said something about his trophy collection? That he wanted to put it away or donate it but his sister would never forgive him if he got rid of it?

What if...

What if Simone took really nice photos of all his awards, got them printed on high quality photo paper, and put them in a nice leather-bound album? Then he could donate all his rodeo trophies to his high school or a rodeo museum or something (apparently they existed), and yet still display them but in a very classy sort of way.

"I'm a genius," Simone said to herself. Best idea ever.

Until she tried picking up one of the cups.

"I'm an idiot," Simone said to herself. But she managed, finally, to heft the big cup and carry it into the spare room photo studio. Prize by prize, Simone set it up against her backdrop, took a photo, and carried it back to the bedroom where she'd found it, until she had them all captured inside her camera. A big undertaking but worth it. After all, for three nights she'd gotten to live in Jason's old white farmhouse, eat his food, ride his horses, and generally have the time of her life. Whether they decided to see each other again or not, Simone thought giving him an album would be a nice way to thank him for the excellent hospitality he'd showed both her and her pussy.

While Simone was thinking about her pussy, she texted Jason a picture of it.

Five minutes later he walked into the house.

Simone sat on his sofa in his living room drinking a cup of tea and trying to look very, very innocent.

"Hello, sir," she said smiling at him. "You're back early."

"Are you trying to kill me?" he demanded.

"What do mean?" she batted her eyelashes.

He held out his phone. "Ahem," he said.

"Have you never had a woman text you a picture of her pussy before?"

"No!"

"Oh. I thought that was standard procedure these days. Want some tea?"

She held out her cup to him, still half full. She smiled. He didn't.

"You're in so much trouble, little girl," he said.

"Oh," she said again. "That a 'no' to the tea?"

"Up." He snapped his fingers and jerked his thumb at the door. Simone set her teacup and saucer on the table. She stood up and walked to the door to the kitchen.

"Are you going to spank me in the kitchen?" she asked.

"No, you'd like that too much."

He was right. She would like that too much.

"Are you going to spank me in the barn?" she asked as he held out her boots. Apparently they were leaving the house.

"I'm not telling you what I'm going to do with you," he said. "I'm keeping you in suspense."

"That's psychological torture," she said. "Good idea."

With a hand on her arm, he escorted her from the house toward the barn. She was having a very hard time not laughing or smiling. She could tell he was, too, though he was doing his level best pretending to be furious at her.

"So I guess I'm not allowed to send you pussy pics?" she asked. "I'm only asking for future reference, sir."

"You can send them when I ask for them, and I

promise you I'm not going to ask for them when my farm manager is standing two feet away from me."

"What? Does Franco not like pussy pics, either?"

"You're gonna get cropped so hard tonight you won't be able to sit for a week."

"I don't really need to sit. Being sedentary is bad for you, I hear."

"I should have known better than to let a pink-haired menace into my house."

"You really should have, sir. Haven't you seen the public service announcements?"

"You could at least pretend to be sorry, Spanky," he said.

"I would if you could pretend to actually be mad about it, sir."

That got him to smile. And not just smile—he stopped dead in his tracks, grabbed her around the waist, pulled her hard against him, and kissed her. It was a good kiss, a hard kiss, the kind that ended with one of his hands in her hair and the other on her ass. When he released her from the kiss she pretended to faint just so Jason would grab her and hold her tight.

"Are all pink-haired kinky girls as crazy as you are?" Jason asked.

"No, sir," she said. "It's just me."

"Thought so. Come on. We're going for a little ride."

"Car ride? Truck ride?"

"Horse ride. We need to see how Cupcake does on a trail. You game?"

"I'm game."

In the barn, Jason outfitted her with a riding helmet and leather gloves.

"I'll walk her," Jason said. "You just—"

"Sit there and look pretty?" Simone asked.

"Right. And I want you to hang on tight, too. The trail twists and winds and goes over some rocks. Long as you sit up straight and stay relaxed, we'll be fine."

Simone greeted Cupcake the way Jason had taught her, by extending her hand for the horse to sniff, then standing at the side of her head for pets and scratches.

Jason saddled Cupcake quickly and led her out to the paddock. This time Simone was able to get on Cupcake without any sudden vertigo. Franco was there already by the gate. Jason had Cupcake by the lead rope and Franco gave her a salute and a smile as they headed toward the dense copse of trees that bordered Jason's farm.

"You know this isn't much of a punishment for sending you unsolicited pussy pics. I love riding Cupcake and hanging out with you."

"When did I say I was going to punish you?" Jason asked.

"Well...I guess you didn't. You just said I was in trouble."

"You are in trouble and you're probably going to stay in trouble for the rest of your natural life. I'll punish you tonight. I thought maybe we should talk a little first."

"Talk?" Simone tensed, suddenly nervous. Almost nothing good ever came of the words *we should talk.*

"Talk," Jason said.

"Okay, sir. Talk away."

"Not me. You. You tell me what you've been thinking about us."

"Is that an order?"

"Yes."

"I was afraid of that," she said. Simone decided telling him she was falling in love with him was probably a bad idea.

"You can tell me anything, you know," he said. "I told you things I never told anybody. I'd like it if you could trust me, too."

"I do trust you. I just don't know if I trust me." They passed into the woods and Cupcake carefully picked her way along the dirt trail. The bright April sunlight shone through the tall trees. If she hadn't been so nervous, she'd be having the time of her life.

"What's that mean?" he asked.

"Oh, you know," she said, trying to sound airy and unconcerned. Meanwhile she was shaking in her boots. "We've only known each other a few days, and I leave tomorrow. And it's really easy to get attached to someone you've been having great sex with, you know...but can you trust those feelings? Or is it just good sex and infatuation? Or something more? And can you ever really know that, or is it the sort of thing you have to wait and see? But since I'm leaving maybe it's all a moot point anyway and—"

"I want to see you again," Jason said simply.

Simone replied immediately. "Yes, that's exactly what I was thinking, too."

Jason brought Cupcake to a halt and turned around to face her.

"You mean that?" he asked.

"Yes. I texted Mistress Nora today to tell her how I was upset I had to leave tomorrow since I...I really like you. Sir."

He nodded slowly.

"This is going to complicate both our lives. You know that, right? If things work out, this can't end with me moving to New York."

"No, I know," she said. "But I travel anyway for my work. One airport gets you there the same as any other. What about you? How complicated can it get for you?"

"Pretty damn complicated," he said.

"Because of your family?" she asked.

He nodded. "We'll cross that bridge when we come to it," he said. "Just this one thing—if you were really mine, like for real, and someone tried to take you from me...I wouldn't let them. I want to keep you, Simone. If you'll let me, I'd like that very much."

Simone's chest heaved. She blinked and wasn't surprised to find tears in her eyes.

"I want you to keep me," she said softly, nodding so he'd know she really meant it.

"Good," he said.

"What do you want to do?" she asked. "I mean... what do you want me to do next?"

"I been thinking about that. My sister's coming to visit with the girls next week for a few days. Once she's gone, my schedule's clear through August. You can come back whenever you want. Sooner the better. And I'd like you to stay with me as long as you can. We'll go from there."

"Sounds good," Simone said. "I'll check my calendar."

"Good." He smiled up at her. "Good."

He set out walking again, leading Cupcake down the winding trails. Meanwhile, Simone's heart floated a few feet above her head, following her like a pink balloon on a string. And it followed her all the way into a line of trees at the edge of Jason's farm. White wildflowers sprouted from thick green grass and a little trickle of water, not even wide enough to be called a creek, wound past them. They were so deep in the little woods she couldn't see his house anymore. Jason tied Cupcake's lead rope to a tree branch.

"Why are we stopping?" Simone asked. Jason didn't answer. He just crooked his finger and Simone dismounted. The second she'd landed on her feet he took off his cowboy hat and hung it on the horn of the saddle before pulling her into in his arms. He pushed her gently back against a tree and now she knew exactly why they'd stopped.

She didn't speak. He didn't, either. No words necessary in a moment like that. Their tongues met in a rough kiss that never seemed to end. Jason's hands slid up her sides to her bra, pushed the cups down and covered her breasts with his warm hands. Simone moaned in pleasure as he lightly pinched her nipples, tugged them, yanked up her shirt so he could lick and kiss them. She ran her hands over his strong broad back, his neck, through his hair. She was leaving tomorrow, and she wanted to touch him and keep touching him until they had to be pried apart. Jason apparently had the same idea.

He pushed her leggings and panties down to her ankles and cupped her between her legs where she was warm and getting warmer. He stroked the seam of her pussy as she pushed her hips into his hand. She grew wet, wetter, and he entered her with two fingers. She looked down and watched him touching her. Her heart clenched at the sight. Simone knew then she never wanted any other man to touch that part of her ever again. Only Jason, now and forever.

"Simone," he said. That was all.

"Jason," she said. And that was all. Their eyes met, then they kissed again.

Jason only broke the kiss to unzip his jeans and push them down his thighs. The condom was on in seconds, and then, right there against the rough bark of the tree trunk, he made love to her. His thrusts were deep, slow and deep. He held her upper thighs in his hands as she lifted her legs off the ground and wound them round his lower back. Her arms wound round his neck. They were joined as hard and tight as the tightest knot ever tied in the tautest rope. Jason pumped into her and she took his cock with pleasure and with joy. He wanted to be with her. He wanted her to come back and stay with him, as long as she could, he'd said. She wanted to come and she wanted to cry. Turns out it was easy to do both at the same time when the master of her dreams was making love to her five minutes after telling her he wanted to keep her.

She shuddered in his arms and if it wasn't the strongest orgasm she'd ever had, it was the sweetest. Jason pumped his hips harder into her and the bark of the tree bit her through the fabric of her shirt hard enough she knew it would leave marks. Good. She wanted to be marked by this moment. She'd remember it the rest of her life—she'd remember Jason's ragged breathing, the way his fingers dug deep into her soft skin, his thick cock sliding in and out of her slick vagina...She'd remembered the way his head fell back when he started to come and his muscles tensed and he took a breath in and didn't let it out for a good long time as his hips pushed and pushed and pushed into her...

As he came Simone kissed his long exposed throat,

and a low groan escaped his lips. She'd remember that, too.

Seconds later it was all over. As Jason pulled off the condom, Simone said, "You know, while we're apart for the next few weeks we could maybe both get tested and then we wouldn't have to use those anymore."

Jason met her eyes. "I'd like that," he said. She would, too. To feel him inside her, nothing between them, to have his come in her...oh yeah, she'd like that.

"And maybe," she said, "when I come back I can bring all my equipment with me—my kink equipment, and you could try flogging me and stuff?"

He nodded. "I'd like that, too."

"And um...maybe, if I have your permission, Master Jason," she said, "maybe it would be okay if I fell in love with you?"

Jason fell silent, completely silent. All she heard in those five long seconds between her question and his answer was the breeze blowing through the new buds on the tree branches, water trickling over stones, and Cupcake ripping grass from the ground by the mouthful.

A smile spread across Jason's face, wide as the blue Kentucky sky.

"Yeah," he said. "I'd like that most of all."

16

Simone had only been gone for two days and Jason already couldn't stop counting the minutes until she came back to him. Watching her drive away yesterday morning had been a bigger punch in the stomach than Demented's horn in his guts. He'd wanted to follow her to the airport, see her off, kiss her until the final boarding call. But she'd asked him to let her go alone. Otherwise, she'd said, she would cry forever.

And he'd rather face Demented again than give Simone cause to shed a single tear.

Unless she was crying from pleasure or a good hard spanking. Those were the only tears he ever wanted to give her.

Jason spent the days after Simone left practically living with the horses in the hopes of staying occupied enough he didn't go nuts until his girl came back again.

He wasn't sure if it was working, but he had to try. At least he had Aimee and the girls coming to visit for a few days while Aimee's husband was out of town on business. They always managed to distract him from whatever was on his mind. And he needed all the distractions he could get if he was going to survive until Simone could visit him again.

Simone hadn't been able to give him a firm date only because she had several bookings that were still up in the air for May. She took her work seriously, and he admired that about her. He was old-fashioned enough he didn't mind the idea of his future wife quitting her job so he could support her. Thanks to Mr. Ford and Mr. Levi, Jason had more than enough money in the bank to keep a roof over their heads for the rest of their lives. But he also had nothing but respect for Simone's career. If she wanted to keep working as a photographer, he'd do whatever he could to help her along.

As for the other career, well, that he would ask her to quit. If anyone was going to be spanking or flogging her, it was going to be him. He didn't think she'd object to that. She'd already canceled the few appointments she had scheduled in that realm, and without him asking her if she would. It seemed they were thinking along the same lines.

Jason strode into the barn on the fourth morning after Simone had left, smiling to himself at that morning's text message exchange. He'd woken her up with an eight a.m. text, and his innocent "Good morning, Spanky" quickly turned X-rated when he asked her to tell him what she was wearing in bed and she replied with "nothing." Photos were sent back and forth and before it was all over both of them had come.

Never ever had he done that sort of thing with any woman. Even when he'd wanted to, he hadn't had the guts to suggest it, afraid of coming off like a sleaze or a creep. With Simone, he lost all his inhibitions, and he had to say, he didn't miss them one bit. On the outside he still looked and acted the same.

Alone with Simone, he was a different man entirely. A better man, maybe, than he used to be. He certainly felt like more of a man now that he wasn't living with a weight of shame hanging around his neck. Simone had taught him that what he liked wasn't for every woman, but it was for her, and if a girl like Simone—sweet, playful, hard-working, and smart—liked it then it must be all right. And if *it* was all right then *he* was all right.

Jason went straight to Cupcake's stall and laughed when the pony stuck her head out, gave a disappointed *pppbbbst* and stuck her head back in the stall.

"What am I? Chopped liver?" Jason asked Cupcake. He went in and started brushing her down. "I know. I miss Simone, too. But you got to get over her. You're getting a girl all your own today. Katie's coming. Let's get you looking good for her."

Cupcake shook her mane but soon settled down

and let him finish grooming her and picking her hooves. Katie and her parents were already on the way over with their rented horse trailer. He got Cupcake saddled and fancied up with a big pink bow around the saddle horn. He led her out into the paddock just in time to see a lanky eleven-year-old girl in jeans and boots running awkwardly down the path toward them, her mother and father chasing right behind her.

Jason brought Cupcake to the rails and Katie was there in a flash, standing on the bottom rail and leaning over to reach for Cupcake.

"Cupcake, you remember Katie, don't you?" Jason asked. "This is your new girl. You want to say 'hi' to her."

Jason always marveled at how quiet a little girl Katie was. His two nieces couldn't stop talking to save their lives. But just because she didn't talk much didn't mean Katie wasn't speaking volumes right then. Her brown eyes were round as quarters and she grinned a huge gap-toothed smile. And when Cupcake bumped Katie's outstretched palm with her velvety nose, Katie squealed with utter delight.

"That's Cupcake saying 'hi' to you, Katie girl," Jason said as her parents came to the rails and watched the show. "That's how ponies say 'hi.' They don't talk much either. But if you wanted to say 'hi' to Cupcake, she'd sure like that."

Katie blinked a few times and took a few nervous breaths, her little forehead furrowed in concentration.

"Hi, Cuppy," Katie whispered. Her mother put her hand over her mouth and tears ran down her eyes. Her father tried blinking back tears but they ran down his face. Jason even had to look away long enough to wipe his eyes.

With her father's help, Jason got Katie into the saddle. Jason led, and Katie's father walked alongside with his hand on Katie's thigh to keep her from falling. Katie was in high heaven, laughing and gasping and calling Cupcake's name over and over again. And Jason could have sworn Cupcake was holding her head a little higher than usual, as if to say, "See? She loves me already."

It would have been perfect if Simone had been there. God, Jason wanted her there so bad it hurt. She needed to be here with her camera, catching every second of this big day on film so Katie and her parents could watch it over and over again. His longing to have Simone there with him was a physical ache, a hunger pain like he hadn't eaten in a week. And he knew she would have loved to have seen all this—Katie's parents cheering her after she dismounted, Cupcake butting her head again and again into Katie's hand, and the joyful shriek of Katie's laughter when Cupcake licked the horse cookie off her palm.

Jason loaded Cupcake up in the horse trailer, knowing as he did that Katie was watching the entire time, inspecting him to make sure he didn't hurt her new best friend.

"She's all yours now, sweetheart," Jason said as he locked the trailer doors. "You take good care of her."

"What do we say to Mr. Waters, Katie?" her mother said.

Katie nodded her head twice as if trying to push out the words. But they did come. Took a few seconds but they came.

"Thank you," she said in her tiny little voice.

Jason felt a fist in this throat but he smiled through the pain.

"You're welcome, Katie," he said. The trailer drove away and there was Franco, handkerchief out and blowing his nose loudly into it.

"Allergies," Franco said.

"Yeah," Jason said. "Same here."

After Katie and her parents left with Cupcake, Jason felt the longing for Simone hit him twice as hard as before. He did what he always did in times of high emotion, when it was either work it out or scream it out. He saddled up Rusty and took him for a long ride through the woods. The woods weren't Jason's. Not all of them, anyway. But his neighbors had a hundred wooded acres that the local horse folk were always welcome to use. Jason and Rusty went over every inch of those hundred acres on that May afternoon, talking it out, thinking it out. By the end of it all, Jason decided there was only one thing to do—admit that he was in love with Simone and stop trying to pretend he wasn't. It wasn't like it was unheard of for two people to fall in love this fast. His own sister said she knew on her first date she was going to marry her husband. "When you know, you know," Aimee had said. Back then, Jason had thought Aimee was a little crazy. Now he knew exactly how she felt.

When you know, you know.

Jason knew.

He rode Rusty out of the woods and along the long road that led from the Paris Pike highway to his farm tucked two miles down the lane. As he and Rusty were heading back to the house, a car pulled alongside him and the window rolled down.

"Need a lift?" Aimee asked.

Jason pretended to peer into the car windows.

"Can you fit me and Rusty in there?"

Aimee had rented a small SUV. His two nieces Dani and Cassie now rolled down their windows and both of them stuck their heads and hands out to pet Rusty on his long nose.

"Can we ride with you?" the twins asked.

"You two can ride and I can walk," he said. "Mom has to drive."

In no time, Jason had gotten all the hugs one man could ever ask for from his sister and two sweet little nieces who were as starry-eyed about horses as their mother ever had been. He led Rusty home with both girls sitting on the big horse's back. They did a very good job of behaving themselves. It helped that Aimee was watching them like a hawk.

"They really should have their helmets on," Aimee said as the car rolled along at a brisk five miles an hour.

"You never wore one when you rode at their age," Jason reminded her. "Explains a lot, don't it?"

"Very funny," she said. "Girls, this is a special occasion. You're always supposed to wear helmets when riding."

"We know, Mom," the girls said without enthusiasm.

"Is that what you say?" Aimee asked.

The girls got the hint quickly. "Yes, ma'am," they said.

Jason only smiled to himself. Aimee caught him mid-smirk.

"Don't you smirk at me," she said. "You gotta teach 'em manners young, or they'll never learn."

"You just sounded so much like Mom it gave me a flashback," he said.

"We're doomed," she said. "You're gonna be Dad, and I'm gonna be Mom. Soon as you have kids, mark my words."

"I am not going to be like Dad," Jason said. "My kids are gonna like me."

"You know you love Dad," she said.

"Love and like are two different things," he said.

Aimee didn't argue. She knew better.

As soon as they got to the house, the girls just had to meet all the horses right that very second. Jason let them. Horses, like all domestic animals, needed to be socialized around children so they'd behave even when little girls squealed without warning. He put all three of the horses out in the paddock and brought horse cookies to the girls.

Jason hung back with Aimee and watched with pleasure as both girls cooed and oohed over his horses.

"If they'd come this morning," Jason said, "they could have met a Welsh pony I was training. Hate that they missed her. She went home with her little girl."

"It's fine," Aimee said. "They aren't picky. If it's got a mane and four legs, they're in love."

Jason only grinned to himself. Unfortunately, Aimee caught him again.

"What?" she asked.

"Nothing."

"You have a girlfriend."

He turned and stared at her, wide-eyed.

"Oh my God, you do have a girlfriend."

"How do you do that?" he asked.

"I know a shit-eating grin when I see it," she said.

"You said a bad word, Mommy," Dani said.

"I'm allowed," Aimee said. "Pet your horses and close your ears. Uncle Jason and I are having grown-up talk." Aimee faced him. "Tell me everything right now this minute," Aimee said in a low voice.

"I have a girlfriend," Jason said and then said nothing more.

"And?"

"And that's all you need to know."

"Maybe that's all I need to know but that's not all I want to know. What's her name? How old is she? Where'd you meet her? What's she like?"

"Simone. My age. At the library. She's sweet. Good enough?"

"Not even close. Is it serious?"

"Hope so."

"Got a picture?"

"None you get to see."

"Jason Thomas Waters, you tell me about your girlfriend and you tell me right now."

"Uncle Jason has a girlfriend?" Cassie asked. She and Dani looked at each other in excitement bordering on horror. The girls had begged him to get married so they could be flower girls. But they were still young enough to fear new things and new people.

"He does," Aimee said. "And her name is Simone and she's very sweet but we're not allowed to see pictures of her so she must be very, very ugly."

"I swear to God, I will make you sleep in the barn tonight," Jason said.

He took his phone out of his pocket and, shielding it with his hand, found a fully clothed photo of Simone. He'd taken a selfie of the two of them with Cupcake after that last ride together. They were both smiling hugely in the photograph. Even Cupcake seemed to be smiling.

Jason showed the photo to Aimee and then the girls.

"She has pink hair," Dani said in wide-eyed wonder.

"Yes, she does," Jason said. He started to put his phone back into his pocket when Dani reached for it. He immediately pulled his hand back and held his phone up in the air out of the reach of little innocent girls.

"I want to play with your phone," she said.

"No way," Jason said. "Not a chance."

"You have better games on your phone than Mom," Dani said, already done with talk of grown-up things like girlfriends.

"My phone is off-limits," he said. "Go pet the horses."

With a groan of disappointment the girls returned to the paddock fence.

"You used to let the girls play with your phone," Aimee said.

"There are things on here they don't need to see. Or you," he said, eying her pointedly.

"Trust me, I saw enough last time I was stupid enough to touch your computer."

"Your own fault for being nosy."

"Not my fault you were looking at things you shouldn't be looking at."

"Grown man, sis."

"You're still my baby brother."

Jason decided to drop the subject but he could tell from the look Aimee gave him the conversation wasn't over.

Unfortunately, he was dead right about that. After putting the girls to bed that night in the guest room, Aimee came down to the kitchen, grabbed a beer out of his fridge and sat across from him at the table where he'd been browsing horse sales on his laptop.

Aimee stared at him. And stared at him.

And stared at him.

"Say it," Jason said, closing his laptop.

"Say what?"

"Whatever it is you've been storing up all day waiting for a chance to say to me. Get it out so I can get back to work."

"These belong to you?" She pulled Simone's pink thong out of her jeans pocket.

"Jesus," he said, snatching the panties out of her hand.

"Found those in the guest room under the bed when I put the girls' suitcases in there. Lucky I found them before the girls did."

"Forgot," he said. "Sorry."

"Hope you changed the sheets."

"Yes, I changed the sheets. Well, Simone did before she left."

"I guess she likes everything pink."

"What's wrong with pink?"

"Just trying to imagine you taking a pink-haired girl with a nose ring home to Mom and Dad."

"Mom's got her ears pierced. So do you. And if they care about what color a girl's hair is, they got too much free time."

"Where'd you meet her again?"

"I told you. In the library."

"So she's from here?"

"No, she lives in New York," he said. "For now."

"For now? You two that serious already? How long have you been dating this girl?"

"A couple weeks."

"Two weeks?" Aimee looked horrified. Jason was not impressed. "That's it?"

"She spent four straight days and nights here. And we talk every day on the phone for hours. She's the one."

"The one? After two weeks? Have you lost your damn mind?"

"You said you knew on your first date you were going to marry Brian, and I thought you'd lost your damn mind. Was I wrong?"

"That's different."

"How you figure?" Jason asked.

"Brian doesn't have pink hair for starters."

"He should," Jason said. "It would look real good on him."

Aimee took a slow breath. She sounded like a leaking tire.

Jason waved his hand at her. "Go on. Lay it on me. I know you don't approve. Might as well get it all out."

"I'm just not sure about this girl," Aimee said. "I just am not at all sure about her."

"Guess what? You don't have to be, because you're not the one dating her."

"Look, I'm not picking on her because she's got pink hair and a nose ring. I couldn't care less about that. I would give you the third degree about any girl you date. Especially if I don't know a thing about her."

"You know everything you need to know and everything you need to know is...she's my girlfriend. The end."

"You're not taking me seriously," she said.

"No, I'm not."

"You used to take me seriously. Is this girl trying to get you to forget you have a family?"

"This girl is named Simone, and she hasn't said a word about my family except to say the girls are cute, and Mom and Dad must be very proud of us. Real crazy stuff like that."

"She tell all her friends she's dating you?"

"She told *one* friend about us."

"So she's already bragging?" Aimee asked. She seemed determined to twist every innocent thing about Simone into something ugly and mean. Jason was not going to let her get to him. He was not.

"Hope so," Jason said. "A man likes being bragged about by his girlfriend."

"Jason."

"Her friends are not followers of the PBR circuit, Aimee," Jason said, trying not to talk down to her though the temptation was mighty. "They live in New York City. The only bull they ever seen is that big fake one on Wall Street. So if you think she's some kind of groupie, think again. I showed her a clip of my run-in with Demented, and she burst into tears. Safe to say my rodeo career is not the attraction here."

"Then what is, can I ask? Your money?"

"She lives in New York City. She probably makes more money than I do to pay those kind of rents."

"What's she do for a living?"

"Photographer. And some odd jobs." Jason thought that was a fair thing to say. Being a professional submissive was about as odd a job as riding bulls for a living. "And a little modeling."

"Oh, she's a model. Now everything is clear."

He glared at her. "Your brother likes a pretty girl. Are you really shocked by that? Come on, Aimee. Use your brain. I've modeled, remember?"

"What kind of modeling does she do? Catalogs and stuff?"

"If you must know, she's a corset model."

"She's an underwear model?"

"Sort of. If you consider corsets underwear."

"Sweet Lord, you are trying to kill Mom and Dad, aren't you? This girl is a double heart attack waiting to happen."

"They won't have heart attacks if they don't look at the pictures," Jason said. "And if they go looking for them, it's their own fault if they find them."

"Is she into...whatever?" Aimee gestured at his laptop.

"That is none of your business."

"So that's a 'yes'?"

"It's a 'that's none of your business.'"

"Well, it's about the only thing you two have in common, isn't it?" Aimee asked.

"That's also none of your business."

"If you marry this girl it's going to be my business," she said.

"And why is that?"

"You think I'm going to let my girls stay in the same house where *that* goes on?"

"I don't know if you know what 'that' is," Jason said.

"I know enough to know I want no part of it, and you shouldn't either. I thought Dad taught you better than that."

"He taught me to be scared to death of my own father, is what he taught me."

"Do I have to remind you about all the kids who look up to you? Including your own nieces? You're a hero to lots of kids who'd be heartbroken to find out you weren't what they thought you were."

"I'm retired," Jason said. "They can look up to Justin McBride and Adrian Gonzales now. And I'm done talking about this with you."

"Fine, be like that," Aimee said, standing up. "You have all the fun with this girl you want. But that's your thing. I don't want that stuff happening anywhere near my girls." She paused and then shook her head. In a much softer voice she said, "I love you more than life itself, baby brother. When you were in the hospital, and they thought you might lose a kidney, I said, 'Give him one of mine.' You didn't need it, but I would have given you a kidney, a lung, a liver, every drop of blood in my veins to save you...You know this is coming from a place of love, right?"

"Right. I know." He did know. He really did.

"It's just...you used to date such sweet girls."

"Simone *is* a sweet girl."

Aimee looked at him with nothing but love in her eyes. "I just don't want to see you getting hurt when she decides she'd rather keep living her wild life in New York than settle down with you in the middle of nowhere." She patted his shoulder and walked away.

Jason stared at nothing for a good long time.

17

Being in love was the best. It really was. Simone wondered why she didn't fall in love more often. Her skin was clear. She had a spring in her step. A cab had nearly run over her just that morning, and she'd only laughed and sashayed away. Nothing could hurt her. She was in love. She was bulletproof. Above the skyscrapers the sky was cerulean blue. The birds were singing arias in Central Park. New York was a city of magic and light, and she couldn't wait to leave it as soon as humanly possible.

And though she considered herself a feminist in every way, shape and form, she found it unbearably fun to write "Simone Levine Waters" on every single scrap of paper that happened to pass in front of her. But she always threw them away before anyone saw.

Although it did have a nice ring to it...

And things kept getting better. The booking she

had for next week—a three-day stint in the Hamptons to photograph a bridal shower, high tea, wedding reception, and the wedding, had been canceled. The bride had dumped the groom and run off with his best friend. It was a massive clusterfuck; everyone was freaking out, deposits were been forfeited and tearful phone calls were being made, and Simone couldn't stop smiling. She wasn't heartless, but this meant she could go back and see Jason again in two days. Two days! Two days too long but still better than the two weeks she'd been thinking it might be.

Plus, better to find out before the wedding that the bride had the hots for the best man than after, right? It all worked out in the end.

Simone bought two days of groceries and took them back to her apartment. She'd always liked her place, small and cramped as it was. She'd decorated it with shabby chic white wicker furniture with lacy white curtains and a pink dust ruffle on her full-size white bed. The living room was frilly, too, painted white with a framed poster of a rainbow over her fake fireplace mantel that hadn't worked since before World War I. As cozy as she'd made it, there was no denying it was a single gal's apartment. There was barely room enough for her in the minuscule galley kitchen, much less two.

As cute as it was, Simone didn't want to spend the rest of her life living alone in a tiny one-bedroom apartment, even if it did have an exposed brick wall and the original crown molding. She was ready for a change, ready for a serious relationship that was going somewhere. A home. A partner in life. Maybe kids someday. She hadn't even realized how much she wanted it until Jason had offered her a glimpse of a future with him in Kentucky.

Simone hadn't just bought groceries while she was out and about. She'd stopped in at a bookstore and picked up a travel guide to Kentucky. Seemed like a nice enough place to live, bit conservative but she'd loved shocking the straights, so why not? Kentucky had two big cities—Louisville and Lexington—and good airports. Two hours on a plane would get her to Orlando. Two hours on a plane would get her back to NYC. Perfect. Plus, she did like the horses. It appeared there was an entire industry down there dedicated to equine photography. She could do that. If she owned a horse she'd want a picture of it hanging on her wall. Who wouldn't?

"You've lost your mind, Simone," she said to herself as she put away her groceries. She'd told herself she could call Jason with the good news but only after she'd put the pint of Ben & Jerry's Urban Bourbon in the freezer. Jason was important, but he wouldn't melt.

But she hadn't lost her mind, she knew. What she'd lost was her heart. The second Jason had given her permission to fall madly in love with him, she had. And the best part was...she wasn't scared. Not a bit. Because Jason was such a good man—steady, strong and stable—that she knew it was safe to love him. Maybe things wouldn't work out. Maybe they wouldn't end up married with kids and living happily ever after on his farm. But she knew in her heart that if things didn't work out, it wouldn't be for lack of trying, lack of love or lack of basic human decency.

Finally, Simone finished putting everything away. She went to her bedroom, threw herself down on the covers and called Jason. Usually they texted during the day and he called her at night before they both went to sleep but this was a special occasion. Plus, she needed to make sure he'd be home during her days off. She was his good little slave, after all. She wouldn't do anything without permission first.

Jason picked up after only two rings.

"Hello, sir," she said.

"Hey," Jason said.

Hey? Not Hey, Spanky? Or Hello, baby? Just hey?

"Is this a bad time?" Simone asked.

"Ah, well, my sister and the girls are here. We're about to go for a ride."

Mystery solved. There were vanilla family members afoot. That's why he was playing it so cool.

"Right this second? This won't take long."

"Go on."

"I had a cancellation. A big one. So now I have a week off between gigs. I have a reception tonight, a christening tomorrow and then I can leave on Monday to come see you. I could stay five whole days. Would that work?"

There followed a pause, a long one. Simone tensed.

"I need to get the flights if that works," she said. "But if you need to check your calendar or something—"

"Well, it's like I said. My sister and the girls are here."

"I'd love to meet them."

"I don't know about that."

"You don't think your girlfriend should meet your sister and her kids?"

"The girls are little, only six. I don't know if...I mean, they're too young to know about certain things."

"Jason, I'm not going walk around the house in a corset and nothing else if other people are there. Or talk about what my favorite floggers are with your sister. I have manners, you know."

"I know, I know," he said and sighed. "It's just...complicated."

"Are you ashamed of me?" she asked. She sat up and pulled her knees into her chest.

"No. It's not that. It's not that at all."

"Then what is it? You asked me to be your girl-friend. You used that word—'girlfriend.' I thought that's what I was. And I thought meeting family members was a pretty normal part of being a girl-friend. If your sister is really religious or something, I get it. I can sleep on the couch if she's uncomfortable with you having me in your bedroom with her kids in the house."

"Not much point in you coming to visit if you have to sleep on the couch."

"I don't know. We don't have to have sex all the time. I just wanted to see you, hang out with you. Even kinky people like curling up on the couch and watching Disney movies."

Simone was suddenly sick to her stomach, sick to her heart. Tears pricked her ears. "Are you having second thoughts about us?" she asked.

"Simone, I—"

"You are."

"I just...there's two little girls in the house, and I can't help but think about how I want to have kids of my own someday and—"

"I want kids, too. I always have."

"I'm having trouble with the idea of being who I am with you and then, you know, looking my nieces in the eyes. Or my own girls someday if I have them."

"Kinky people are allowed to have families," she said. "They're just like vanilla couples. They don't have sex in front of their kids. Adults are allowed private lives. Even parents."

"Can you maybe give me a little more time to think about this?"

"You said we'd cross this bridge when we came to it," Simone said. "Those were your words. Now we're at the bridge, and you're telling me you don't want to cross it?"

"Please," he said. "Can I just have a little time to figure out if this is right for me?"

Simone wanted to say "yes." She wanted to say he should take all the time that he needed. But she couldn't. She couldn't let him sit there and think there was something gross or wrong or weird or creepy about what they were. Yes, she loved him, but no, she was not going to let him treat her like some sort of deviant who had to be kept away from children and gentle ladies.

"No," Simone said. "You either accept that there's nothing wrong with what you and I *both* are and you do it right now or you end it with me like a man. What'll it be?"

"Simone, all I asked for was a little time. I told you there's a lot of little kids that look up to me and—"

"There is nothing wrong with what you and I do alone together in private."

"Tell that to the world."

"No, because it's none of the world's fucking business," she said. "I gave my answer. No, you don't get more time to decide if I'm a decent person or not. You do not. Not one minute. Not one second. Because I am a good person and so are you. At least I thought so before this conversation."

"You're awfully demanding for a slave," he said.

"And you're pretty weak-willed for a master," she

said and ended the call before she said anything else she regretted.

She stared at her phone in her hand. Had that phone call really happened? Did Jason actually tell her he didn't want her around his little nieces?

Too stunned to cry, too shocked to move, Simone sat on the edge of her bed for what felt like hours. Only when the alarm on her phone buzzed obnoxiously, warning her she had to leave for her job tonight did she get herself moving again. The job. The gig. Photographing the wedding reception. Right. Simone focused on her work because if she didn't, she would collapse in tears on the floor and there'd be no getting her up again.

The reception was a casual affair being held at The 8th Circle, the kink club where the couple had met and Simone occasionally worked. The wife, Tessa, was a rope bunny and a bondage fetish model. She and her husband Eric wanted some fun, classy bondage pictures of the two of them together for an album they were planning on calling "Tying the Knot." Simone changed out of her jeans and t-shirt and into a little black corset dress and high heels. She gathered all her equipment and hailed a cab.

Half an hour later Simone was at the club. The reception was being held in one of the large dungeon spaces. A table was stacked high with a black wedding cake, fresh fruit, cheese and wine. Electric votive candles burned inside dozens of Chinese lanterns hanging from the ceiling. Someone had even strung pretty Christmas lights from the suspension beams. It was all very sweet and lovely and romantic, and it made Simone want to find the nearest bathroom and throw up for an hour.

But she didn't. She pasted on a fake smile, mingled with the guests, laughed during the X-rated toasts, and took fantastic photographs of Eric tying up Tessa, suspending her from the ceiling beams, and feeding her cake and kissing her all while she was upside down, Spiderman-style.

When they finished with pictures, Simone decided to fake a stomach ailment and bid everyone a very early goodnight. She was just about to leave when she heard a laugh, a familiar laugh, big, sexy and brassy. Simone turned around and saw her friend Mistress Nora standing in the doorway of the dungeon. She was talking to Tessa, the bride, and giving her a gift, a square black box wrapped in a red ribbon.

"It's a human head," Nora was saying to Tessa as Simone came up to them.

It was such a relief to see Nora, Simone's knees wobbled. As soon as Nora spied her, she threw her arms around Simone.

"What are you doing here?" Simone asked the beautiful, black-haired woman she hadn't seen in months.

"You know I'll take any excuse to come back to New

York. What's up? You look paler than usual, kid," Nora said.

As much as Simone wanted to tell Nora everything, she knew there was nothing the woman could do but commiserate. What she needed was to speak to a man about this, a man who might understand Jason's fears. Simone sure as hell didn't get it.

"I know this sounds weird," Simone said, "but would it be okay if I called Mister S and talked to him? I'm having master trouble."

"Ooh," Nora said, as she picked up her wine glass off the table. "Master trouble is the worst sort of trouble to have. But I wouldn't call him if I were you."

"Why not?" Simone asked.

Nora pointed with her wine glass at the tall, blond, imposing man striding down the hallway toward them. He wore a black suit, crisp white shirt, and black tie.

"Because he's right there," Nora said. "He's my date."

Simone kissed her on the cheek quickly and ran out into the hall. As soon as Mister S saw her, he smiled.

"Hello, Jellybean," he said. "It's been too long. How are you?"

Simone looked up at him and swallowed hard.

"I..." It was as far as she got.

Simone burst into tears and collapsed against him.

He put his arms around her and held her close as she wept loudly and long against his chest.

"Ah," he said. "Memories."

That made her laugh when she thought nothing could. Yes, she had cried for him a few times when he'd broken her into a million lovely little pieces during a session. Cathartic tears. Happy tears. Laughing tears. Not like these tears. Not broken-hearted tears.

"I need to talk to you," Simone said. "Please?"

"Let's find a room," he said. He guided her down the hall until they found an empty room. He sat in a large leather armchair beside a gas fireplace. Simone threw a pillow on the floor at his feet and knelt there, her head in his lap, his hands in her hair.

"Tell me everything," he commanded softly.

She told him.

18

Jason had taken the call from Simone in his bedroom far away from the prying ears of Aimee and the girls. They were downstairs in the kitchen baking rhubarb custard pie for dessert while he was upstairs kicking himself repeatedly in the ass for how badly he'd handled the conversation.

He wasn't asking for much, was he? A little time to figure out how to be in a relationship like this and also not alienate his entire goddamn family? Seemed like a reasonable request. But Simone acted like he'd insulted her to her face. He would never do that. Never in all his life would he insult a woman to her face. Or behind her face. Or anywhere. He knew for a fact Aimee was overreacting but what big sister didn't when she thought her baby brother was dating someone bad for him. Simone was a fetish model with pink hair, piercings, tattoos, who'd never sat on the back of a horse in her life until he'd put her on one. Yeah, on paper, of course, that didn't look too great. While his father had literally beaten respectfulfulness into Jason, their mother had lectured Aimee on an almost daily basis about how Christian girls were supposed to act. Dress modestly. Act modest. Don't be a stumbling block for boys. Don't tease. Don't be like those girls on TV with their short dresses and too much makeup. So of course it would be hard for Aimee to get used to the idea of him dating a free-spirited girl like Simone. Simone was the exact opposite of the woman Aimee had been raised to be. His family was important to him, even if he didn't always agree with them. He had every right to want to take a little time, not rush things, and ease his family into getting used to the idea of him with Simone.

But if he was in the right and Simone was wrong, why did he feel so sick to his stomach?

Was it because she'd called him weak? Well, that certainly hadn't felt very good. People said things when they were angry they didn't mean. He'd been trying to spare his family's feelings. How was that weak? And of course her feelings were hurt. She'd wanted to come visit him and he'd asked her not to while his sister and nieces were there. The day before he'd told her he was counting the minutes until she could come back again. But after seeing how upset Aimee was about it all, he knew it wasn't time yet to make those introductions.

He was definitely in the right. Right?

Yet the nauseated ache in his stomach remained.

Jason ignored it. He took his phone from his pocket and dialed a number.

"Asshole," was the first word spoken by the person who answered.

"Whatever happened to 'hello'?" Jason asked.

Luke answered, "Hello, asshole. Why you calling me? I'm busy here."

"Busy in the hospital?"

"I'm out, man," Luke said. "Got out yesterday. I'm about to get a sponge bath from a sexy nurse."

"If you're out of the hospital, why the hell do you have a nurse giving you a bath?"

"I asked her real nicely."

"Good Lord," Jason said. Luke only laughed.

"How's your girl?" Luke asked.

"Not very happy with me right now," Jason said.

"Good. Send her my way. If you won't be nice to her, I will."

"I swear to God if you weren't already limping, you would be after this conversation." Jason should have known better than to call Luke. The man had a gift for saying the exact opposite of what Jason wanted to hear.

"Hey, don't take it out on me just because you fucked up. I assume it was you doing the fucking up because otherwise you wouldn't be crying in my left ear."

"It's complicated, all right," Jason said. "Things got kind of serious fast, and Aimee's giving me hell over it."

"Why? She not like pink hair on girls? I like it myself. My nurse has purple hair. It's cute as hell."

"Simone's, you know, a little wild. Well, not for New York City, I guess, but for Montana she's wild. She's my kind of wild."

"I'd kill for a girl who was Montana wild," Luke said and Jason detected a note of real longing in his voice. "I know if I had one, I wouldn't let my stuck-up sister get in the way of us being wild together."

"Aimee isn't stuck-up."

"She's so stuck-up I don't even know what she looks like. I met her a hundred times and all I can picture is the bottom of her nose it's stuck up in the air so far."

"She thinks you're a bad influence."

"I am a bad influence. But you're also a grown man. Last I checked anyway."

"She's just protective of me because of Dad."

"Fact is, man, your sister is not going to like any girl you date unless she's an Aimee clone and you know it. Call me crazy, but I wouldn't want to date my own sister. Not that I have one, but if I did, *hell no*." Luke managed to draw "hell no" out to about ten syllables.

"You're a sick man, Bradley."

"Truth hurts. I'm sure your sister's great to you, but a man has needs his family doesn't need to know about or think about it."

"What would you know about it?" Jason asked.

Luke fell quiet for a few seconds.

"I know a lot about it," Luke finally said. "And I know if I had a girl who understood all that about me, I would not fuck it up a week after meeting her. Now fix it with her so she can introduce me to all her wild friends. I am only two weeks away from being healed enough to fuck again."

"So me making up with Simone is about you, not me?"

"Right," Luke said.

"I'm hanging up now."

"Good. My bath's ready."

Jason hung up.

He shook his head and considered tossing his phone across the room just for the hell of it. But before he could, it buzzed in his hand with a text message.

From Luke unfortunately.

What the hell did that insane cowboy want now?

"Hey," Luke wrote. "I'm going to be serious for two whole seconds. I talked to your girl only two times on the phone when it was supposed to be me in that calendar. When she found out I had to bail because I got hurt, she sent me a get-well card and candy. That's why I was kind of interested in her. Not because she's hot. Because she's sweet. I'm jealous you got someone that sweet when all I get are girls who only want me because they seen me on TV. All I could think about in the hospital was getting out and finding something real for once. Do not reply to this message. Just read it and delete it and if you tell anybody I said all that I'll call you a damned liar."

"God damn," Jason said, reading the message a couple times before deleting it as requested. He didn't know Simone had sent Luke a card and candy. That was pretty damn sweet. And Luke, poor guy. Jason knew exactly how he felt, lying in a hospital bed for days and nights on end, wanting to get out but also dreading the moment he got home again to an empty house.

Jason sat back in his chair and threw his boots up on the desk. Maybe he ought to go for another long ride. Maybe that would help clear his head.

But he already knew it wouldn't. Nothing was going to help except figuring out what to do and how to do it.

Outside Jason heard a loud rumbling sound, heavy tires and air brakes.

Aimee called up to him from downstairs.

"UPS delivery, Jase!"

Grateful for the distraction, Jason went downstairs and signed for his package. He didn't remember ordering anything.

The package was from Simone.

She'd sent it three days ago, long before their fight so he wasn't scared of opening it and finding a bag of dog shit and a nasty note. He didn't want to open it in front of the kids, though, so he went into his office, shut the door, and found his box cutter. He sliced the tape off the heavy rectangular box and nervously opened it.

It was a photo album. Oh God, what sort of X-rated pictures had she sent him now?

Carefully, he opened the front page of the album and furrowed his brow in confusion. It was a photograph of his PBR cup, the big one. The next photograph in the album was of his trophy from winning the Bud Light Cup. And on the next page, a photograph of his medals. In fact, the entire album was nothing but pictures of his awards and trophies and cups and buckles and every other prize he'd stashed in his bedroom. The photographs were all beautifully shot and staged. He could frame them and put them on the wall if he wanted. When he got to the last page, he found a note from Simone—black ink on pink paper.

"My Darling Master Jason,

Now maybe you can donate your trophies to a museum or your high school and still "have" them. I'm as proud of you as I am relieved you're retired. I can't wait to see you again. Being your slave has been the most freeing experience of my life.

Love,

Your Spanky."

19

Simone poured out her heart to her beloved Mister S until she had nothing left to tell him.

"*You're pretty weak-willed for a master...*" Mister S repeated in a solemn tone. "You do go for the jugular, don't you, Jellybean?"

Simone snorted a liquid weepy laugh and blew her nose again on his handkerchief.

"I'm a horrible slave."

"No, no, no," he said gently. He patted his leg, a signal for her to get off her knees and sit on his lap. As soon as she was in his arms, she rested her head on his shoulder, and he held her close like a father. "You can't be in a relationship like that without speaking your mind. And a real master can take it."

"I don't know if he took it or not," she said. "I hung up on him right after."

"For the best," he said. "It's easy in those situations

to say things you'll immediately regret. Silence has its virtues at times."

"Here's the thing, though," Simone said, pulling back to look him in the eyes. "He was fine with me. Just great. Happy. Totally into it. And then—bam!—he just decides that it's all wrong and weird. It came out of nowhere."

"Did it?"

"What do you mean?"

"You told me his family is very conservative, that his father whipped him with a belt for even daring to raise his voice at his sister. He's twenty-nine years old," Mister S said. "Twenty-nine years is a long time to live with a lie in your head. A few days with you, no matter how blissful, might not be enough time to completely dislodge that lie. And the lies our parents tell us have barbs in them. They not only stick, but they tear when you pull them out."

"I just...I'm so crazy about him," Simone said. "I thought we had it figured out."

"If it's any comfort to you at all, I've fallen in love twice in my life and both relationships involved long difficult separations. Even when it's meant to be, it isn't necessarily meant to be *easy*."

"But I really want it to be easy," she said and collapsed onto his shoulder again.

"Don't we all, Jellybean." He patted her back and she sighed. At least Mister S loved her and that was something special.

"What should I do?" she asked.

"Nothing," he said. "You've made up your mind. You know how you feel about him, how you feel about the both of you as a couple. You can either wait for him to make up his mind, or end it completely with him and move on. You can't force someone you love to be someone they aren't. Take it from me."

"I just want him to be who he was when we were together. I think his sister must have got to him. When she found out he watched some kinky porn, she told him to get therapy."

"I'm sure she received many of the same toxic messages he did growing up under that roof," he said. "And if they're close, he'll take what she says to heart whether he should or not simply because he loves her and trusts her."

"I thought he loved me," Simone said. "A little anyway."

"The new lover versus the family," he said. "One of the older battles in human history."

"I want to win," Simone said, raising her fist in determination.

"I know you do. And you might," he said, pushing a pink lock of hair off her face and tucking it behind her ear. "You were his first submissive, first woman he ever hit. Even when it's consensual, hitting a woman is a harrowing experience for any man with a conscience. I would counsel you to give him the grace of a few days to process the strong emotions he's undoubtedly feeling. I would ask him to do the same for you were the situation reversed, give you enough time to deal with your conflicted heart. You remember how badly you wanted to quit graduate school, but you were afraid of disappointing your mother? You were dying to quit but stayed in your PhD program for her sake for another miserable year."

"Ugh," Simone said. "Don't make me empathize. I hate that."

Much as she hated to admit it, he was right. She'd been where Jason was, wanting something for herself but ignoring her own better judgment, her own passions, because she loved her family so much and couldn't bear to disappoint them.

Mister S lightly pinched her thigh. She sighed again and rested her head on his chest. He patted her back gently, like a father tending to a tired child.

"It might be for the best," he said after a long silence, "that it ends now, early, before you grow any more attached than you already are."

"You think so?" she asked, sitting up in surprise.

"You and Jason have so little in common. I can certainly foresee a painful breakup in the future if you stayed together."

"Really?" His words broke her heart.

"I'm afraid so. I've seen it too many times to count."

Her bottom lip quivered but she tried not to cry again. She nodded slowly. "You're probably right. We... we don't have a lot in common, really."

He smiled. It was a wicked smile. Positively satanic.

"What?" she asked.

"You see how easy it is?"

"What do you mean?"

"You care about me. You trust me. Although you were certain of your feelings one minute ago, I was able to plant a seed of doubt in your brain with just a few barbed words. This is how it happens when someone you trust and care about makes you second-guess your own heart."

"You did that to me on purpose?" she asked, staring at him in wonder and horror.

"Of course I did."

"You're evil."

"I proved my point."

She lightly beat her head against his shoulder. "Evil. Evil. Evil," she chanted. He only laughed.

"So you don't think Jason and I are bad together?" she asked him.

"If you say you are a good couple, I believe you. You've always been a thoughtful, rational person. Even when your hair isn't."

Simone smiled.

"Sweet-talker. I can't believe you messed with my head so easily. No, wait, yes I can."

"Are you feeling any better?"

"A little," she said. "I don't want to scream anymore."

"Let's go and have a glass of wine, and we'll take

you home after. You'll feel better in a few days once you see the world hasn't ended."

"You're so smart and wise."

"Yes, I know."

"Pretty arrogant, though."

"Well aware, Jellybean. Well aware."

20

Jason sank down into his office chair and flipped through the photo album over and over again.

It was the sweetest damn thing any girl had ever done for him, making him this photo album. And it was smart, too. Completely solved his problem of what to do with that mass of metal in his bedroom. He picked up her note again and read it. She'd not only signed it with a heart but she'd kissed the paper with dark pink lipstick. He ran his fingers over the kiss and ached inside like he'd never ached before. He ached so hard to be with Simone again he opened his laptop and pulled up the video they'd made together. But he didn't watch them having sex. He forwarded all the way through that to the very end. There they were lying on the bed. He was on his back, Simone was on his chest. They'd forgotten to turn off the camera and he was glad they hadn't. The camera caught the look on Simone's face when he put his arms around her. She closed her eyes and smiled like a girl in love. He had to see that smile again. Now.

Right now.

"I'm a goddamn fool," he said out loud because he deserved to hear it.

Without giving it one more thought, Jason closed out of the video, opened up the internet and started looking for a flight that would get him from Kentucky to New York tonight.

There was a knock at the door and before he could say, "Come in," Aimee stuck her head in and said, "Dinner's ready."

"Eat without me," he said. "I have to go."

She walked in and shut the door. "Go where?"

"New York."

Her eyes widened. "What? Why?"

"Because I need to go apologize to Simone."

"For what?"

"For listening to your bullshit and taking it out on her."

"Jason!"

He spun around in his chair and looked at his sister. He pushed the photo album toward her. "Simone just sent me that. Look at it," he said.

"Do I have to?"

"Look at it," he said. He must have sounded serious because she opened the front page. "You see all that?

She did that for me. I told her I was sick of having all my trophies underfoot and wanted to donate them to the rodeo museum. She took those pictures of every single one of my trophies so I can donate them and still keep them. Isn't that the sweetest damn thing in the whole wide world?"

"It's very nice," Aimee conceded. "But that doesn't mean you should run off and marry this girl. She's about the last girl on earth Mom and Dad would want for you."

"Don't care."

"What?"

"Don't give a shit. Not a single solitary shit."

"Jason, you don't mean that. You can't possibly want an underwear model as an aunt to your nieces."

"This is coming from a place of love, Aimee. But that's your problem, not mine. They're your kids. You feed them all the 'good girl' garbage Mom fed you if you want. I'm out. I don't care if Simone walks down the highway naked, she's still the best thing that's ever happened to me. And I'm going to go, right now, to the airport and pray to God the whole way there she forgives me. And if she does, I'm going to throw her over my shoulder and bring her back here with me. And if you're here when we get back, you better straighten up and treat her with the respect she deserves. And if you can't do that, then you better be long gone or I'll kick you out on your ass in front of the girls if I have to."

Aimee was red in the face, ready to blow her top. He could not begin to care.

"You are really going to pick this girl you barely know over your mother, your father, your sister, and your nieces?" Aimee demanded. "You're not. I know you're not."

"Fuck yes, I am," Jason said. Except he didn't say it.

He yelled it. And God damn, it felt good.

And on his way out the door he stopped, looked at his sister, and grinned.

"And you know what else?" he said. "She's not the only one who's modeled naked. I have, too."

"What? When?"

"For a charity calendar, and I am completely naked in it. I'll send you the calendar for Christmas. Everybody's getting one for Christmas, and when you see my bare ass in that calendar, feel free to kiss it. Then maybe y'all will stop trying to make me into a saint when all I ever wanted to be was my own man."

He left at that because he was going to be his own man.

But first he needed his girl.

21

Simone had a glass of wine with Mister S and Mistress Nora. When she reached the bottom of her glass, she was feeling mostly okay again, thanks to Mister S (and Mrs. Merlot). Mister S and Mistress Nora shared a taxi with her and Mister S even walked her all the way to the front stoop of her building.

"You'll be all right?" he asked her.

"I will," she said.

"Give him time," he said again softly. "I've been in his shoes. I never want to wear them again."

"Thanks for everything," she said and rose up on her tiptoes to kiss him on the cheek.

"Simone?"

She gasped and turned. Jason stood on the side-walk, hat in hand and staring at her in shock.

"Jason?"

She glanced up at Mister S who seemed to be trying not to smile.

"That didn't take long," Mister S said under his breath. Then he slowly drew himself up to his full height. She saw his expression alter slightly from one of concern to one of cold-blooded, dead-eyed sadism.

"Behave," Simone whispered to him.

"I'm sorry to interrupt, Simone. Sir," Jason said, and Simone admired him for the quick recovery of his manners.

"Not interrupting," Mister S said, his voice calm and cold, an assassin's voice. Poor Jason. "Shall I walk you up, Simone?"

"I'm fine," she said. "Thank you."

"Goodnight, Jellybean. Call if you need us." He bent and kissed her cheek. Then he met Jason's eyes and simply looked at him. She had a brief flashback to the movie *Terminator*. Same expression. Jason took a step back. Mister S walked on.

When they were alone, Jason took a step forward into the light of a street lamp.

Jason. Here. At midnight. On her street. What on earth...

"So...that him?" Jason asked.

"That's him," she said.

"He's, um..."

"Tall? Handsome? Scary?"

"I felt like I needed to salute him or something. Should I have saluted him?" Jason asked.

"He wouldn't have minded," Simone said.

"Glad he didn't take a swing at me. Think I'd rather ride Demented again than tussle with that old boy."

She smiled. "He's my friend. Doesn't mean he's your enemy."

"Did you tell him that?"

"He's just messing with you," Simone said. She was so relieved Mister S had been there for her. Now she could have this conversation without falling to pieces at the mere sight of the man she loved more than anything.

"I guess, you, ah...you spent time with him," Jason said.

"I needed to talk to someone about you. I was upset. He helped me feel a lot better."

"I thought that was my job," Jason said.

"Yeah, well, you weren't here."

"I am now."

"Why?" she asked. Her voice was steady but inside she quaked with fear and excitement, but mostly fear. If Jason was really the good guy she thought he was, he could be here for a couple of reasons. Either he wanted to make up. Or he wanted to break up, and he felt obligated to do it to her face and not over the phone.

"Katie and her parents picked up Cupcake," he said.

"Was she happy?" Simone asked.

"Cloud nine, ten, and eleven," Jason said. "And you should have seen Cupcake strutting around like she'd invented strutting. Katie even said a few words. God, we were all in tears. Even Franco. Even me."

"I wish I could have been there," Simone said.

"I wanted you there so bad," Jason said. He took a deep breath. "Then Aimee showed up with her girls and she, ah...she's not too keen on the idea of you and me."

"She hasn't even met me," Simone said.

"Mom raised her as tough as Dad raised me. Be modest. Don't tease boys. Girls who wear tight clothes are just asking for trouble."

"I guess I'm asking for trouble," Simone said, pointing at her corset dress. Then she remembered what Mister S had said about those lies that stick in kids and rethought the sarcasm. "I feel bad for your sister being raised to think there's something wrong with women living their own lives, dressing the way they want and all that."

"I was raised to think more of others than I do of myself," Jason said. "Family first. Work first. Put others before you. Don't be selfish."

"It's a good thing to be selfless," Simone said. "But dating who you want to date doesn't make you selfish. It just makes you an adult."

"With you and me together," Jason said, "there is a real chance my sister and parents won't...well, there's a real chance it could get very ugly, and, um...Aimee said she might not let me see the girls if you and me...well, you know."

"I don't want you to have to choose between them and me. I really don't."

"I appreciate that," he said. "But it's all right. It is what it is. And if it comes down to that, I want you to know something. I want you to know...I'll choose you every time."

Simone's heart jumped so high and hard in her chest that it hit her ribs. She put a hand on her chest as if to keep it from bursting out.

"You will?" she asked, tears springing to her eyes.

"I will, baby. I swear I will. From now on. I will never screw up like I did today again. I got bad thoughts in my head and got spooked. You just get this idea in your head of who people want you to be and you can forget real easy that who they want you to be and who you are, well, they aren't the same person. And you can't be two people so I'm just going to be the man who loves you."

Simone couldn't speak. She could barely even stand.

"Now, I suppose this is when you tell me off," Jason said. "And I deserve it. Give it to me good, Spanky."

Simone would do just that.

She took one step and then the next one and stopped on the bottom step and met Jason eye to eye.

Then she gave it to him good.

She wrapped her arms around his neck and kissed him.

22

This had gone better than Jason had been expecting. He could hardly believe Simone was back in his arms, kissing him and letting him kiss her in return. He'd thought for sure he'd get an earful about how much he'd hurt her, what a fool he was, and how he better never do it again. Either she really loved him or she was the sweetest girl on earth. Both probably.

When she pulled back from the kiss he saw the tears in her eyes.

"I'm sorry," he said. "I never want to hurt you again."

"You came all the way to New York to apologize. I can't...I can't believe it." Her hands were on his shoulders and his eyes searched her face. He couldn't stop looking at her. This girl was his girl and always would be.

"I got the photo album you sent me this afternoon and soon as I saw what it was I knew I'd made the biggest, stupidest mistake of my life. I took the very next flight out of Kentucky."

"Everyone gets cold feet," she said. "And I know it's not easy trying to be who people want you to be. I shouldn't have called you weak. That was mean and I'm sorry. It's not weak to want to make your family proud of you."

"It is weak to let someone else tell you how to live your life when you know better. And I knew better. Old habits die hard, you know. But they're gonna die. I've already started killing them."

"You didn't kill your sister, did you?" Simone asked, eyeing him.

"No, but some words were exchanged," he said, wincing.

"You yelled at your sister?"

"She insulted my girlfriend. Of course I told her off."

"That's pretty sexy," Simone said, grinning.

Jason was happy to hear that.

"And I told her if she couldn't be nice to you, she better not be at my house when we get back."

"When 'we' get back?"

"You don't think I'm going home without you, do I?"

"Well, I can't leave until Monday."

"Fine. You can show me New York. I've never seen it."

"I can do that," she said. "First place I'm going to show you...my bedroom."

As soon as they were inside her building, they kissed. Then they kissed on the first floor landing, kissed a little longer on the second floor landing. He slipped his hand under her little black dress and hiked her leg around his back before kissing her again against the wall, which he would have been happy to do for hours, except an elderly woman stepped out into the hallway with a trash bag in hand, looked at them and said, "Get a room" in Spanish.

"*Lo siento, señora*," Jason said quickly. Laughing, Simone grabbed him by the hand and pulled him to her apartment door.

Jason was happy to see her hand shaking a little as she unlocked her door. He knew how she felt. He was shaking with excitement, happiness, and plain stupid relief she'd forgiven him so easily.

"Cute place," Jason said, glancing around her apartment.

"Want the tour?" she asked. "There. Done."

"Still haven't seen the bedroom."

"It's all the way over here," Simone said. They went five steps and were at her open bedroom door.

"You don't love me," Jason said, glancing at the tiny bedroom that barely left any space between the full-size bed and the wall, window, and door. "You just love my square footage."

"I don't care about the feet," she said, unbuckling his belt. "Just the inches, sir."

He smiled happily, drunkenly. "I missed that 'sir.' Much as I missed this girl."

Before she could reply he kissed her again and while kissing her, pushed her down onto the bed. He stopped only to ask her a very important question.

"Now didn't you tell me you keep some toys at your place?" he asked her.

She grinned and pointed down.

"Under the bed?" he asked.

She nodded, still grinning.

He leaned over the side of the bed, looked under the dust ruffle, and found a box underneath.

"You keep your kinky stuff in Tupperware?" he asked as he pulled out the large flat plastic tote.

"It's a space saver," she said. "You need that in this place."

"Good point." Jason pulled the lid off and could have sworn he heard a choir of angels singing somewhere. In the box were floggers, thin rattan canes, handcuffs, paddles, and rope.

"That's what I'm talking about right there," he said and pulled a bundle of soft black rope out of the box. "This I already know how to use."

"Do you?"

In record time, Jason tied the end of the rope into a

lasso. He spun it once and tossed it over her shoulders.

"Damn, you're good," she said. "Sir."

"What did I say about that unladylike language?" he asked.

"That I'll be punished for using it?"

"Right. So why did you use it?"

"So I'd be punished for using it."

"What am I going to do with you, Spanky?"

"Punish me, I hope, sir?"

"Guess I gotta. You're overdue for it." He pulled the lasso tight around her shoulders and yanked her gently to her feet. He wrapped the rope a few more times around her arms and then bent her over the bed. She sighed with pleasure as he lifted the back of her dress to expose her bright pink panties. She sighed again when he slid them down her thighs. Hard and quick as he could, he spanked her six times in a row until her skin burned bright red.

"That's more like it," he said.

"I'll say."

"Not if I gag you, you won't."

Simone said nothing. Quick learner.

As he held her close and tight in one arm, he ran his hand all over her ass and thighs. He felt her go limp against him, leaning on him completely, trusting him to hold her and not drop her. And he would honor that trust by never ever letting her go.

Again.

Jason stripped her out of her dress and threw her

back down onto the bed. He tied her wrists to the headboard and when she couldn't do a damn thing to stop him—not that she would—he kissed her from lips to ankles and up again, stopping between her beautiful soft thighs. He licked her inside and all over until she was panting for him, begging and dripping wet. Only then did he take off his clothes. He didn't stop for a breath until he was deep inside her with her ankles on his lower back and her breasts in his hands. He kissed her chest. He kissed her nipples. He kissed her mouth all the while moving in her hard and slow, slow and deep. Jason could have stayed in her all night. He planned to. All night and forever.

"Why are you smiling, sir?" Simone asked.

"Because I'm going to use everything in that box on you before morning," he said. "And tomorrow you're taking me shopping and we're going to buy every kinky thing you want and I want and we want. Although..." He paused. "How we're gonna get it all home on the damn airplane is beyond me."

"You just check it," she said. "You can take any kinky stuff you want on a plane in checked baggage."

He pushed up on his arms and looked down at her with narrowed eyes. "How do you know that, Spanky?"

She smiled, and it was the smile that he'd fallen in love with and the smile he was going to stay in love with the rest of his life.

"What can I say?" Simone said. "This ain't my first rodeo."

23

October, Six months later

Simone woke up to a bright Kentucky autumn morning. The sky outside their bedroom window was so blue she had to blink a few times to take it all in.

"Master Jason?" she called out and then yawned hugely. No answer. Jason had already slipped out to do his morning check on the horses. Well, that was fine. She would get up, get dressed, and maybe she'd have breakfast ready by the time he came back. Busy day for both of them. Jason was packing to leave on a two-day road trip to pick up a Quarter Horse in Georgia he'd scouted for a local teenage girl who was learning to barrel race, and Simone was going with him. The horse farm they were visiting outside of Savannah had hired her to take the photographs of all their stock for their website. In just two months' time, ever since packing up her apartment in New York and moving in with Jason, she'd already begun to make a name for herself in the tight-knit horse industry with her equine photography side business. People said she had a gift for capturing a horse's personality with her pictures. She'd already been working on a charity calendar to raise money for Jason's nonprofit, which helped provide therapy animals to kids in need. Every month was a shot of a child with a horse. April, the month she and Jason had met, was for Katie and Cupcake, Simone's favorite picture by far. Mainly because Jason was in it too, at Katie's insistence. The little girl had a big crush on Jason.

Simone couldn't blame her. She had a big crush on him, too. And she had the tattoo on her arm to prove it. A tiny Ps 23:2, a reference to Psalm twenty-three, the second verse, "He leads me beside the still waters..." Jason "Still" Waters approved wholeheartedly of her ink. His family might not, but they were working on that. They'd been almost as angry about Simone as they were about Jason posing nude in the charity calendar. Jason said it was nice to have company on the shit list. He didn't seem worried about it much so Simone didn't worry, either.

In an effort to make peace, Simone had made two copies of the photo of Jason, Cupcake and Katie, framed them, and sent one to Jason's mother and one to Jason's sister Aimee. She'd received a very nice handwritten thank you note from Jason's mother—progress. Meanwhile, Aimee had actually called and said the photo was so sweet it had made her cry. Aimee had even let Simone talk to both of Jason's nieces on the phone. When the girls asked her if she'd take pictures of them with their horses, Simone had said they'd have to ask their mother about that. Aimee said, "Next time we visit." Another good sign.

Jason had told his whole family that he and Simone were together now, and he wouldn't be going anywhere she wasn't welcome. That hadn't gone over very well at first. But now, maybe, it seemed the Waters family was warming up to her. Aimee had even sent Jason a text message saying that she was happy he was so happy.

Maybe by Christmas, they'd actually let Simone into their homes. But if not, she would take Jason with her to visit her family back in Connecticut. Or invite her parents, sister and nephew down here. Or...maybe she and Jason would just spend all December from Hanukkah to New Year's Eve in bed together.

They'd probably go with that last option. They had plenty of holidays ahead of them to spend with family. Simone stood up and pulled on Jason's abandoned flannel shirt from yesterday. He loved it when she slept in his shirts, loved taking them off of her in the middle of the night even more. Simone stood up and stretched, thought about taking a shower, eating breakfast, drinking coffee...that didn't last long. She collapsed onto the covers intending to sleep a few more minutes. But when she rolled over she heard a weird sound, like she'd lain on a pile of paper. She sat up and saw she'd accidentally landed on a large envelope Jason had left laying on the covers. What on earth?

A note on the envelope said, "Open me."

Interesting.

She smiled as she opened the envelope. She loved when Jason was in the mood to play games with her. He'd fully embraced his role as her owner and master, and not a day passed he didn't remind her who was boss in the house. Considering the orders he gave her were things like, "Come for me" and "Suck me" and "Tell me how you want me to fuck you," it was a pretty easy job being his submissive, servant, and slave. She'd never been more content in her life. The only thing that could make her any happier was Jason hurrying back from the barn to spank her again before breakfast. If her ass could take it. She had a nice blue bruise on it this morning. Turned out Jason was a natural with the paddle. Not that she was complaining. Not at all.

Inside the envelope was a calendar. Not just any calendar—*their* calendar. It was the Naked Men Reading Books literacy charity calendar. It had come in the mail to them yesterday, but Jason hadn't let her see the final product. She'd thought he was simply torturing her by hiding it. Now she discovered he apparently had an ulterior motive for keeping it from her.

She flipped immediately to the month of November. Jason was Mister November, after all.

She groaned. The evil man had taped another, smaller envelope over his picture. How rude. If she opened this envelope to find an even smaller envelope inside it, she would scream.

Simone screamed.

Then, very carefully, as it was so small, she opened the third tiny envelope.

Inside that envelope was a tiny card, and on the tiny card were written three words.

"Pick a date."

Pick a date?

Pick a date...

No. No way...he didn't mean *that* date, did he?

Jason appeared in the doorway. Simone looked up at him in shock. She was breathing so hard she thought she might pass out.

"Jason?"

He held out his hand and in his palm was a ring.

"You have to say 'yes,' Spanky," he said. "It's an order."

"Yes, sir," she said, already crying, already shaking, already ready to marry him today.

Then he slipped the ring on her finger and as soon

as she saw it she knew he was the perfect man for her and always would be.

It was a diamond ring, of course. But not just any old diamond.

A pink diamond.

THE END.

Turn the page for "Flogging 101 with Professor S," a bonus short story that takes place two days after Jason and Simone's reconciliation in New York in Chapter 22.

FLOGGING 101 WITH PROFESSOR S

"I'm not sure about this," Jason said as Simone led him to a gunmetal gray door in a dingy parking garage. She pulled a key out of her purse and slipped it into the lock.

She didn't turn the key. Instead she left it in the lock and leaned back against the door, arms crossed over her chest. God bless her, she didn't laugh at him though Jason could tell it was killing her not to.

"Master Jason," she said.

"Miss Simone."

"It'll be fun, I promise."

Jason didn't know about that.

"Will it?" he asked. "You're sure? One-hundred percent sure?" Even if Simone were ninety-nine percent sure, they'd go back to her apartment right now and find something else to do with her body. He had suggestions.

"Remember, I've been flogged before. A lot," she said. "Like...a billion times."

"For work," he reminded her as he slid his hands over her hips. "But alone with me? That's what you really want us to do?"

Simone gave him that little look of hers that said *Poor sweet innocent dominant...*It was like a pat on the head from her eyes.

"You want to flog me, don't you?" she asked.

He glanced away and grinned sheepishly. "You know I do," he said. "But only if you *really* want it."

"Let me tell you something about flogging," Simone said. "It's the best. It starts with you either undressing me or making me undress for you, and there's nothing wrong with that, is there?"

"Nothing wrong at all in the whole wide world."

"Then you have to tie me up with my hands way, way up here..." She stretched her hands high over her head, which lifted her breasts and forced her back to arch. Jason could look at her posing like that all day and night. "And then I'm all trapped there, tied up, which means you can do whatever you want to me, and I can't do anything about it. And the flogging itself? Oh my God..." She took a shuddering breath, pure sex. Even her eyelashes fluttered. She lowered her arms and wrapped them around his shoulders.

"That good?" Jason asked.

"Floggers are like huge hands with dozens of fingers so when you use one on me, it's like having your hands on me, touching and spanking me all over...Flogging makes your skin so alive and sensitive...every touch feels a thousand times...more. Just more." She took another breath as Jason pulled her against him.

"It's all that?" he asked, trying not to smile.

"All that and *more*. It's intimate, like sex, and intense, but it's not sex. So we can have a flogging scene and then we can have sex, so it's twice as much intense sexy intimate fun than what vanilla people do. And when it's good...when it's *really* good," she said as she ran her hands up and down his chest over his gray t-shirt, "then it's like we're the only two people in the entire world. Everyone else disappears, and it's just us, which means we can do whatever we want forever and ever and ever..."

To that whole speech, Jason said only, "Hmm."

"Will you kiss me, please and thank you?" Simone asked.

Jason raised his chin, looked at her through narrowed suspicious eyes.

"I don't know about that," he said.

She fluttered her eyelashes.

"Don't you want to kiss me?" she said, grinning girlishly.

Of course Jason wanted to kiss her. When didn't he want to kiss her? Especially since Simone looked extra-kissable today. She wore her pink hair up in a pink ponytail and had on a short pink and white polka dot dress that hugged all her curves. Pink high heels, of course, and her pink lipstick was just begging to be kissed right off her pink lips.

"Not gonna do it," he said. "I need to keep my head in my head right now, and if I kiss you, you know what I'll be thinking with for the next two hours."

Simone grabbed him two-handed by his t-shirt and dragged him to her. She kissed him on the mouth and before he could stop himself, he was kissing her back hard enough she ended up flat against the door again with one of her legs around his waist.

How on earth did that happen?

Jason forced himself to pull back from the kiss. He kept her leg wrapped around him, though.

"All right," he said, staring down into her smiling face. "I'll do this. But if he gets all uppity with me, I'm outta here."

"Mistress Nora's going to be there, too. What if she gets all uppity with you?"

"That I might like," Jason said for the sole reason of riling Simone's little jealous side up. It worked.

Her mouth fell open and Jason took that as an invitation to kiss her again. Open mouth, tongue fit right in.

Simone moaned with pleasure and Jason knew if they didn't stop soon, that other leg of hers was going to find its way around his back. They'd fucked against a door before, just last night in her apartment when they couldn't wait to get to her bed. Good thing her old apartment had sturdy doors, because he'd gripped her ass so hard he'd left bruises on both cheeks while he rammed into her pussy until she'd come with a cry into his ear and by God, he would do it again right here in this parking garage if she made him.

"Ahem."

A woman's voice had made that "Ahem." Jason was so surprised by it, he almost dropped Simone. Luckily, he managed to recover quickly enough to lower her leg to the ground before he turned around and faced She-Who-Had-Ahemed at them.

He knew Mistress Nora on sight. He'd seen her picture, her video, but they hadn't done justice to the woman in front of him.

She was Simone's opposite in a way. Simone was all pink and playful today. Mistress Nora, however, had black hair that hung down in wild waves around her face. She wore tight black pants, black high heels, and a black corset top. She was even looking at them over the top of her black sunglasses. The only thing on her not black was her blood-red lipstick on her full lips.

"Hi, Mistress Nora," Simone said. She giggled and wiped her mouth with the back of her hand. "You look like a vampire."

"Thank you, darling. Had a midnight session with some rock god, or so he tells me. Haven't changed clothes."

"Anyone I know?" Simone asked.

"You ever heard of Nine Inch Nails?" Mistress Nora asked.

Simone jaw dropped again. "Yeah?"

"It wasn't him," the mistress said.

Simone playfully shook her fist at Mistress Nora. "Sadist," Simone said.

"Ma'am, I'm Jason," Jason said. He thought he better introduce himself. Mistress Nora gave the impression she was a woman who liked men to mind their Ps and Qs.

"I figured," Mistress Nora said, shaking his hand. Firm grip for a woman with very delicate hands. "Let's go in. Blondie ought to be here any minute."

"The singer?" Jason asked.

"Mister S," Simone translated for him. Right. Mister S was blond. Jason hadn't noticed the man's hair color as he'd been too busy not being murdered by the guy two nights ago.

"Wagons ho," Nora said as she snapped her fingers and pointed at the door.

Jason turned the key and opened the door for Simone and for Mistress Nora as well.

As the mistress passed him at the door, she paused, looked him up and down over the top of her sunglasses again and said casually, "If you break her heart, they'll never find your body."

Jason swallowed. "I guess you know people," Jason said, trying not to look terrified. Mistress Nora seemed like the sort of gal who knew "people."

"No," she said. "I *am* people."

With that she sashayed into a long corridor. Jason took a deep breath and followed the women inside.

"You have interesting friends, Spanky," Jason muttered into Simone's ear.

"Isn't she fun?" she asked. Jason didn't answer.

They walked down the dimly lit hallway on faded red paisley carpeting past old wood panel walls. Tarnished brass chandeliers hung from the ceiling. It was ten in the morning and it seemed they were the only ones in the building.

"What is this place?" Jason asked as he took Simone's hand.

"Old hotel," Mistress Nora said. She led the way while he and Simone followed her into the labyrinth of corridors. They went down a short staircase, through a set of doors into another long hallway. "Used to be called The Renaissance. Then it was sold, almost condemned. Then Kingsley—"

"That's my old boss, Mister K," Simone explained.

"King bought it," the Mistress continued. "It's been The 8th Circle for years now. Very hard-to-get-into kink club. Unless you know somebody who knows somebody, you probably won't get in."

"Good thing I know somebody," Jason said and squeezed Simone's hand.

"Two somebodies," Mistress Nora said, raising two fingers and smiling. "Having an obscene amount of money will also do."

Mistress Nora brought them to a door at the end of the hallway. She knocked once and opened it when no one answered.

"Welcome to the junior dungeon," Mistress Nora said as she waved Simone and Jason inside the room.

"Junior dungeon?" Jason said as he stopped in the doorway.

"Because you're a little junior dominant." Mistress Nora pinched his cheek. Jason allowed it. He didn't like it. But he allowed it.

"It's the training dungeon," Simone said as she slipped past him and into the room. "Has all the basics plus good lighting."

"And the library," Mistress Nora said as she walked to one of those fancy glass-front bookcases on the far wall. Jason saw it was packed with nothing but guides to BDSM play. Not all books, though. Quite a few DVDs as well. He might like to watch a few kinky DVDs. For educational purposes only, of course. "This was my idea. But if you check out a book, you better return it. We fine in floggings."

"Nora makes a very sexy vicious librarian," Simone said. "I've seen it with my own eyes."

"I can picture that," Jason said and promptly pictured that.

"Picture what?"

The question came from the doorway. The question came, specifically, from the tall blond man standing in the doorway. He wore jeans, a black shirt with sleeves rolled to his elbows, and he carried a long black bag over his shoulder.

"Nothing," Jason started to say. "Not a thing."

"Jason was picturing Nora as a sexy librarian," Simone said. Jason glared at her. He hoped there were gags in this training dungeon.

"No, I wasn't," Jason said.

Mister S only said, "Why not? I would if I were you."

Then Simone's mysterious Mister S did something Jason never expected the man to do.

He laughed.

Simone put her arms around him and went up on her tiptoes to kiss him on the cheek. Mister S dropped the bag on the floor before turning to kiss Mistress Nora on the lips.

"Wait," Jason said, pointing at Mister S. "Has he actually been nice this whole time, and y'all just been messing with me?"

"No," Mistress Nora said. "Definitely not nice."

"Not really," Simone said. "But he's friendly enough when you get him in a good mood."

"And nothing gets *him* in a good mood faster than being spoken about as if *he* weren't standing right here," Mister S said, and pointed at the floor.

"Sorry," Simone said.

Mister S poked her nose. "You are not."

"True."

"Shall we get started?" Mister S said. "Our flight's

at one."

"Sure," Simone said. "I just wanted Jason to get a Flogging 101 lesson from a couple of experts. So... Master Jason, Mister S, Mistress Nora...flog away."

"Can I call you something other than Mister S?" Jason asked. He felt kind of weird calling a grown man the same kinda goofy nickname his girlfriend called him.

"S is for Søren," Mistress Nora said. "Danish. S, O with a slash, R, E, N. Almost rhymes with Burn but put an extra U in there. You sort of have to hold your lips weird."

"Forget it. Mister S is fine," Jason said. He wasn't sure he could hold his lips weird enough to say "Søren" correctly.

Mistress Nora said, "Or *Professor* S. He really is a college professor. I suppose that makes me his T&A."

"T.A., Eleanor. They're called T.A.s," the professor said. Mistress Nora winked at Jason.

Jason ignored both Mistress Nora's wink and her T&A.

"Professor? For real?" Jason asked, skeptical. "What of?"

"You wouldn't believe me if I told you," Professor S said as he made a circuit of the room, inspecting the premises and the flogger selection, it seemed.

Jason said, "Try me."

The professor looked at Jason. "Pastoral studies."

Jason closed one eye, left the other open, thought about that long and hard.

"Yeah, I don't believe you," Jason said. "But Professor S at least sounds official."

"'Sir' would work as well," Professor S said.

"Behave," Simone said and lightly swatted his stomach.

"I don't want to," the good professor said to her. Simone furrowed her brow at him and made the meanest, angriest face Jason had ever seen her make. She hissed like a snake. It worked. Professor S folded. "Fine," he said. "I'll behave. But only for you, Jellybean."

"All right, all right." Jason interposed himself between the two of them, his hands up. "Enough. You —" He pointed at Mister/Professor S. "Stop calling my girlfriend cute names. That's my job. You—" He pointed at Simone. "Don't go making mean faces at people and hissing likes snakes when they're trying to help me out. And you—" He pointed at Mistress Nora.

"What about me?" Mistress Nora asked, her head slightly tilted to the side and a feral smile on her face. Her voice was pure velvet, pure seduction. It was the last voice you heard right before the knife slipped between your ribs and into your heart.

"Nothing," Jason said immediately. "I have nothing but respect for you, and I just want everyone present to know that."

"He's a keeper, Simone," Mistress Nora said.

Simone wrapped her arms around Jason's waist and kissed his neck.

"I agree."

"I'm going to flog someone now," Professor S said. "Volunteers?"

Simone raised her hand. Jason took her arm by the wrist and lowered her hand.

"I'll do it," Mistress Nora said. Jason could have kissed the woman. But respectfully only, and not on the mouth. Just the hand. Maybe one finger. The pinky. The tip of it.

Without any hesitation at all, Mistress Nora began to undress and nobody seemed to mind. In fact, Professor S didn't pay much attention to his lover getting her top off as he was too busy with the big black bag he'd set on a table. He'd unzipped the bag and went digging through it while Simone looked on.

"Jason," Professor S said.

"Yes, sir?"

Simone gave him a look.

"I said 'sir' because I was raised to be polite and respectful to my elders," Jason said. "Not because he's a whatever. Dominant."

"And sadist," Professor S said.

"That," Jason said. "What am I doing?"

"You see all those floggers on the wall?" the professor said, nodding toward the almost two dozen different floggers hanging on hooks along the wall.

"I see 'em."

"Pick one."

"Which one?" Jason asked.

"Anyone you like. Try them all. Test the weight. Tug the tails. One will feel better than the others in your hand. That will be the flogger you should train with. Then you can experiment with other types when you're more proficient."

"Simone said you're really good with the big buffalo floggers," Jason said.

"I'm also six-foot-four and two hundred ten pounds," Professor S said. "And you are?"

Not. Jason was *not* six-foot-four and two-hundred-ten pounds. He was five-eleven and one-seventy pounds wet. As a bull-rider he didn't usually feel intimidated by other men. This was a new experience for him. As lean as Professor S was...Jason knew that two-ten had to be all muscle.

And ego.

"I've ridden twenty-five hundred-pound bulls," Jason said.

"But did you flog them?" Professor S asked.

"Søren," Mistress Nora said.

"It was a reasonable question," Søren said. He winked at Jason. Suddenly Jason knew he was among friends.

Very, *very* strange friends.

Simone helped Mistress Nora out of her corset top while Jason tried to pay attention to anything but Simone helping Mistress Nora out of her corset top.

When he plucked the first flogger off the wall, a black one with supple tails and a light easy weight, Jason felt a jolt of pleasure and power run through his body.

"Oh, yeah," Jason said as he slapped the tails of the floggers against his calf. "I'm going to like this."

"I knew you would," Simone said. Her voice was full of champagne bubbles. She was having as much fun as he was. "You can play around with all of the different types, and then we can go shopping later when you know what you want."

All of them. That's what Jason wanted. He picked up flogger after flogger—red ones and blue ones and ones with sharp tails and knots in the ends and ones with tails soft as suede.

He picked up one and laughed, recognizing the material of the tails immediately.

"This is horsehair," Jason said.

"Very itchy," Simone said. "Very stingy. But fun."

"I could probably make my own horsehair flogger just from brushing Rusty's tail. Although," Jason said. "That would be weird."

"I don't think Rusty would mind," she said.

Jason took a flogger off a silver hook and as soon as he held it in his hand, he knew he'd found the one.

The grip was red and black braided leather and the weight was heavy but not too heavy, the tails supple but thick, the whole thing a little over two feet long. It felt good in his hand, felt like it belonged there, like he'd been born to hold it, wield it, whip it.

"This one," Jason said. "I like this one a lot."

"Let me see," the professor said. Jason held it up. Simone giggled.

"What?" Jason asked to her laugh.

"Of course you like it," Simone said.

Professor S explained, "It's a bull-hide flogger."

"Hmm..." Jason said, nodding. "I wonder if I've ridden his cousin."

"Can we get started, please?" Mistress Nora asked. "I'm getting chilly."

Mistress Nora stood naked from the waist up facing the big black leather St. Andrew's Cross. Her wrists were strapped to the tops of the X. He enjoyed, more than he would admit, watching Simone standing behind the mistress, pinning her long hair up and off her back. Jason could have watched The Mistress Nora & Simone Show all day.

"We're starting," the professor said. "Jason, come. Bring your flogger."

Jason walked over to the cross where Mistress Nora was waiting. Simone had also pinned a white towel to the wall several feet away from the cross.

The professor pointed at Mistress Nora's long lovely naked back.

"That," he said, "is what I'll be flogging. That—" Professor S pointed at the towel, "is what you'll be flogging."

"Understood," Jason said. Nobody started bull-riding by riding a bull. Better to start out hitting a towel than hitting a person.

"The first thing you need to know about flogging," the professor began, "is that a flogging doesn't begin with a flogger. It begins here."

He held up his hand and placed it gently on Mistress Nora's back. She shivered and smiled, and Jason could swear he saw her visibly relax. Her head went down and her eyes fluttered closed and for a split second she almost looked submissive and happy about it.

While the mistress had a large presence, the second Professor S's large hand lay on the center of her small back, Jason saw she actually wasn't a very big woman. Petite, really. And yet she'd been putting up with this giant blond brute for years supposedly. As they said down in Kentucky, God bless her.

The professor stroked Mistress Nora's back over and over.

"You want to touch the person you're flogging first," the professor said. "Establish contact, comfort them, warm their skin, relax them..."

"I can do that," Jason said. He could already picture playing this game with Simone now.

"And talk to them," the professor continued. "Flogging isn't a punishment, but a pleasure. It's not something you do *to* someone. It's something you do *with* someone. Many dominants will thank their submissives for playing with them. The top can ask how the submissive is feeling, what they're feeling, what they want to feel..."

"Or," Mistress Nora said, "if you're old like we are and you've been doing this forever, you're lucky to get a 'Brace yourself' before the blows start."

"Do as I say," Professor S said, grinning, "not as I do."

Jason smiled as Professor S dropped a quick kiss on Mistress Nora's shoulder. They could pretend to be old and over it as much as they wanted, but Jason could tell real love when he saw it. They were crazy about each other. Jason and Simone were going to be just like that ten, twenty years from now, too.

"If you were to visually represent a flogging," Professor S said, still stroking Nora's back, "it would look like a long mountain chain with a series of ever-increasing peaks and plateaus. You start on the ground and work your way up a bit in intensity, then stop and rest. Let her rest," he said, nodding toward Simone who stood back, watching intently. "Let yourself rest. A tired top is a dangerous top. You don't want to lose control of your aim. Rest and check in. You can do as Eleanor does and ask 'What color?' when she's flogging."

"Color?" Jason asked.

"Red means 'stop'," Mistress Nora said. "Yellow means 'slow down.' Green means 'Go, go, go.' It's a quick easy way to check in and make sure things aren't getting to be too much for your sub."

"I only have two people in my life now that I ever flog," Professor S said. "And I know them well enough we don't have to stop and check in that often. If I go a little too far with Eleanor, I know she'll say something to the effect of—"

"Asshole!" she said.

"Not that 'Asshole' counts as your safe word," Professor S said.

"Yeah, usually at the point I'm yelling 'Asshole' is about when I start having fun," Mistress Nora said.

"You don't get to yell 'asshole' at me," Jason said to Simone.

"Dickhead?" Simone said.

"Master Dickhead," Jason said. Simone blew him a kiss.

"Now for the actual mechanics of flogging," the professor said. "We'll focus on the three basic throws. A single throw, a figure eight, and a whip throw. Are you ready, Eleanor?"

"Hit me," she said.

Jason watched intently as Professor S demonstrated how to hold the flogger handle for a single throw, then with a shockingly sudden flick of his wrist, slapped Mistress Nora's right shoulder with his flogger. A red rose bloomed on her back.

Mistress Nora hadn't even flinched.

"That was a single throw for obvious reasons," Professor S said. "One throw, one hit. Now figure eight

—you'll be hitting the spot twice, once coming in high with a forehand, low with a backhand."

Professor S demonstrated, hitting the same red rose on Mistress Nora's back with impressive accuracy.

"If your submissive or bottom prefers a stinging sensation, then you'll want to use the whip throw," Professor S explained. "Hold the tips of the tails of your flogger like this..." He stood with the handle in his right hand, the tips of the flogger in his left hand, "And snap."

Professor S snapped the flogger against Mistress Nora's back so hard she jumped and so did Jason.

"Asshole!" Mistress Nora muttered.

Now they were having fun.

"Your turn," Professor S said.

Jason turned to his towel. Here goes nothing, he thought.

He threw the flogger and hit the towel in the lower corner.

"Stand back," Professor S said. "Square your shoulders. Aim higher. This is the green zone..." He ran his hands over Mistress Nora's upper back, her ribcage area. "This is the red zone." He ran his hands again, now over her kidney area. "When you get very good, this is also in the green zone." He ran his hands over Mistress Nora's shapely ass and thighs. When he came back up, he pinched that very shapely ass very hard. "No kidney area. No stomach. No face, no neck, no arms, no chest—"

"Unless you're a dominatrix," Mistress Nora said. "Then you can whale on whatever body part you want because you're being paid gobs of money by extreme masochists to beat them into the ground."

"I'll stick to the back for now," Jason said. He spent the next half hour flogging the towel as Professor S offered suggestions, corrections, and then... finally...*finally*, a single compliment.

"Good aim," the professor S said as Jason successfully hit the same corner of the towel ten times in a row.

"I've been throwing lassos since I was four," Jason said. "Lots of practice aiming."

"When the flogging session is over," the professor said, "you'll want to engage in aftercare. Take her down off the cross gently and carefully. Flogging can—and should—cause an endorphin rush. She might be dizzy so help her down. After that, water and rest. Ask how she is. Spend time together."

"Or," Mistress Nora said, "if you're old like we are, you fuck hard and then immediately roll over and go to sleep."

"That works for me, too," Simone said. Jason looked at her. "Just saying."

"Now what?" Jason asked the professor.

"Rest and then go again." Professor S said that as he uncuffed Mistress Nora from the cross.

"On me," Simone said.

"What?" Jason asked.

She grinned, kissed his cheek, and said, "Go again on me."

"I'm kinda new at this," Jason reminded her.

"Yes, but I'm not." Simone batted her eyes at him.

"Could you tell her this is a bad idea?" Jason looked at the professor while pointing at Simone.

"She's your partner," Professor S said. "If she trusts you enough to let you try on her, you should trust her judgment. You're not hitting hard enough yet to harm her. Go easy and at worst, you'll mess up her hair."

Simone said, "My hair can take it."

Mistress Nora quickly laced up her corset top.

"You'll have to start trusting her and yourself eventually," Mistress Nora said.

"I'll try it," Jason said. "But supervise, okay?"

Simone stood facing the enormous X of the St. Andrew's Cross. Jason hung up the flogger, went to her and unzipped the back of her dress. He lowered it to her waist. It was easy enough to cuff her wrists to the cross, but not so easy to step back away from her warm soft skin.

Then he remembered not only was he allowed to touch her, he was supposed to. He rubbed her back from shoulder to shoulder, shoulder to hips and up again and all over. Simone sighed, smiled and Jason smiled to himself. Nothing made Jason happier than making his Spanky happy.

He leaned in close and put his mouth as her ear.

"You're everything I never knew I needed," Jason said. "What do you have to say to that?"

"Hit me, Master Dickhead," she said. Jason roared with laughter. God, he loved this girl. He kissed her shoulder again and Simone whispered, "I love you, Master."

If he hadn't been in the mood to flog her before that, he was now.

He stood back and waited for Professor S to give him the nod of approval.

Yes, he was standing in the right spot. Yes, he was holding the flogger correctly. Yes, he was ready.

Jason said a quick prayer that he wouldn't hurt Simone in any kind of bad way.

Then he took a deep breath and threw the flogger at her right shoulder, quickly but carefully. It hit her, but not hard. Jason was thrilled to see he'd struck exactly where he'd aimed. He did it again, hitting the same spot. Then again, a little harder, and her pale shoulder turned pink.

Jason thought he'd only flog her a dozen times, if that, just to get comfortable with hitting a person. But he fell into a rhythm, and the flogger fit in his hand like it was made for him.

Simone made little gasps when he struck her, gasps followed by her sweet sexy giggles. He kept going, losing himself into the role of the dominant until it didn't feel like a role anymore, but just him. Just Jason being Jason and Simone being Simone and them being them together.

When his shoulder tired out after a few minutes or an hour—he had no idea anymore—he lowered the flogger, stepped close and stroked Simone's red-warm back.

"This is fun," he said. An understatement. He was hard and in heaven and Simone was pink and panting and as pretty as he'd ever seen her.

"More fun if I was naked," she said.

"Probably, but we got company."

"No, we don't."

Jason looked around and saw that Mistress Nora and Professor S were long gone.

"I told you when the flogging is going good," Simone said, "everyone will disappear but you and me."

"You were right." Jason peeled out of his t-shirt and pressed his naked chest to her naked back. Simone inhaled sharply at the sudden intimate contact, and it was the sexiest sound he'd ever heard. "You were right about something else, too."

"What's that, Master?" she asked.

Jason pulled her dress down her hips and took her panties to the floor with it. He left her standing in nothing but her pink high heels.

"This will be much more fun if you're naked."

He ran his hands up her body, caressing her breasts and fondling her nipples, rubbing her hips and slipping two fingers into her pussy. She was wet and hot inside and his cock stiffened and throbbed. He wanted to fuck her almost as much as he wanted to keep flogging her. Time enough for both.

Jason stroked her clitoris until she started panting. Then he stepped back, picked up the flogger again, and let the world disappear until there was no one left but him and Simone and the flogger.

And a note from Mistress taped to the back of the door that read, "Good job, Asshole."

ABOUT THE AUTHOR

Tiffany Reisz is the *USA Today* bestselling author of the Romance Writers of America RITA®-winning Original Sinners series from Harlequin's Mira Books.

Her erotic fantasy *The Red*—self-published under the banner 8th Circle Press—was named an NPR Best Book of the Year and a Goodreads Best Romance of the Month. It also received a coveted starred review from *Library Journal.*

Tiffany lives in Lexington, Kentucky with her husband, author Andrew Shaffer, and two cats. The cats are not writers.

Subscribe to the Tiffany Reisz e-mail newsletter and receive a free copy of "Something Nice," a standalone ebook novella set in Reisz's Original Sinners universe:
www.tiffanyreisz.com/mailing-list

facebook.com/littleredridingcrop

twitter.com/8thcirclepress

instagram.com/tiffany_reisz

ALSO FROM TIFFANY REISZ & 8TH CIRCLE PRESS

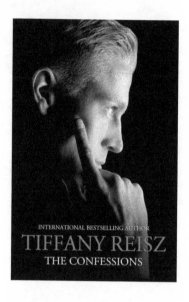

Father Ballard has been Marcus Stearns' confessor since the young Jesuit was only eighteen. He thought he'd heard every sin the boy had to confess until Marcus uttered three words: "I met Eleanor." A moving coda to the award-winning Original Sinners series.

"The reward for the tempestuous journey of all [Sinners readers]…" — Heroes & Heartbreakers

eBook, Paperback, and Audiobook
www.8thcirclepress.com